Faking It
An Across the Hall Novella - Book 1

AJ Claremont

Let's Collective Publishing

www.ajclaremont.com

Edited by Alysha Thornton @athorntonedits
Cover Design: 100covers.com

First Edition: 2026

Contents

To Erik,
my real-life, swoony, cinnamon roll hero.

Chapter 1

Liv

The only thing more relentless than the driving rain outside Bar None tonight is the dude with a man bun who sidles up beside me.

"It sure is coming down out there," he says, smiling as he perches—uninvited—on the barstool next to mine. He's already offered to buy me a drink, which I declined. And asked if I'm staying in the hotel attached to this bar, which I also refused to answer.

I glance up from my drink and nod once at his latest attempt—it *is* coming down out there.

The sky was only a little gray when I left work, and I needed a drink. So I ducked into Bar None, my favorite neighborhood dive bar, to take the edge off the day I'd had. I was supposed to meet my roommate, Andy, but she was nowhere to be seen. Unsurprisingly, Andy wasn't very good at planning, keeping track of time, or remembering either.

I was about to finish my two-block walk home when the skies opened up—and Douchey McDouchebag started hitting on me.

Honestly, getting drenched might've been preferable to getting drooled on.

I glance over my shoulder at the door, hoping to see Andy bound through and save me from this mess. She could shut this guy down in two seconds flat and have him crawling out of here with his tail between his legs—without even breaking her smile.

I could almost hear Andy's voice like Elle Woods. *"What? Like it's hard?"*

"Why the face?" the guy asks, not deterred at all by my silence, and his question sounds a lot like 'smile more.'

I take a long sip of my bourbon and close my eyes. I might fall asleep right on this barstool. Beta launching RootDown's daily habit loop kept me up for thirty-five hours straight. Our wellness startup's latest app gamified sleep tracking. Ironic, since I haven't done it in days. While I usually work from home, I don't think I've set foot in my apartment in weeks. I want to go home, ditch my bra, and binge-watch *Bridgerton* before heading back to the RootDown offices in twelve hours.

"Just a long day." I try to sound pleasant but firm. Andy says I give off grumpy cat vibes in public. She may have also blamed my grumpy cat vibes on my lack of a love life, but I like to think I'm discerning. And this too-close-talker with his whisky breath, is not it.

"We could turn it into a long night." He winks, swiveling his body closer to mine, sliding his hand onto my thigh. My spine goes rigid, and I look down the bar to catch Frankie, the bartender's, eye.

What were you supposed to order if you needed an escort out of the bar? An angel shot?

"Button?" a smooth voice calls from my other side.

You've got to be kidding me. Two in one night? And did he just call me Button? But I turn my head toward the voice. A man in an impeccably tailored suit, his piercing green eyes locked on me, moves toward me with determined purpose.

"There you are," he continues, locking eyes with me and nodding once, barely tipping his chin. "Sorry, I'm late." He slides his hand to the small of my back and kisses my temple delicately. My eyes go wide, but my insides flutter.

The stranger leans around me to my bar companion, who finally has enough sense of self-preservation to remove his hand from my thigh. "Excuse me, do you know my wife?"

Wife?

"Um, no, we were just chatting about the storm," Douchey stammers, "no harm."

"Not yet, at least," my fake husband purrs, closing his hand into a not-subtle fist on the bar.

The man pushes back from his stool and raises both hands in a conciliatory gesture before stumbling away. The stranger lets his hand drop from the small of my back, and I miss the sensation. He rests both elbows on the bar and looks down. Even in the dim light, the faintest blush appears across his cheekbones.

"Sorry," he murmurs. "I hope I didn't overstep, you just seemed..."

I probably should be angry. Who did this guy think he was? What if I liked that guy's attention? What if he ruined my plans for the night? But as the man squirms a little, shifting his weight and refusing to look at me, I can't help but smile.

"It's fine."

"Okay," he straightens and pats the bar twice, "well, enjoy your night." He turns to leave.

"Actually," I add, "thank you."

He turns back and nods again. Something about his face, the sharp angle of his jaw, and the way his eyes seemed like they were lit from within made me want to stay, order another bourbon, and see where the night went. Wouldn't that be ironic? To have this stranger rescue me from one predatory asshole, only for me to turn around and be the overzealous one to proposition him?

Maybe I need my self-preservation to kick in.

"Okay then," I push myself off the barstool and grab my bag. "I think that's it for me tonight."

My savior steps back to let me pass, his eyes downcast, almost embarrassed. My heart cracks a little for him. I stop in front of him, waiting for him to meet my eyes again, then offer a reassuring smile.

"See ya around, husband."

Chapter 2

Owen

What the fuck did I just do?

I watch the beautiful brunette in the pale yellow blouse walk out of the bar without a backward glance. What had I been thinking? We were in a bar, for God's sake. By definition, this is where men hit on women. Why had I thought that she needed to be rescued? I hadn't even heard what that dude said to her. I just watched her back stiffen when his hand slid to her thigh, and some goddamn primal instinct to protect took over.

It was like when I was a kid and my mom finally agreed to let us get a dog. My two older sisters fawned over the puppies at the animal shelter, but I sat next to the scared, older dog until she finally trusted me enough to leave the corner. Then I staged a dramatic sit-in, knowing if we didn't take Bella home, no one would.

Kind of like dramatically pretending to be a stranger's husband in a bar.

That wasn't my original plan; I was just going to ask if she was okay. But I couldn't help but notice how her nerves seemed to relax as I got closer, like she knew I was there to help.

I'd seen that same nervous energy when I met Eli, and something told me he just needed somebody who believed in him. I convinced him—a no-name author—to take a chance with me—a no-name agent—and two years later, he won a goddamn Pulitzer.

So sometimes my instinct paid off. Although, unlike the brunette, I hadn't been wildly attracted to our old dog Bella or Eli.

I slump onto the barstool and try to get the bartender's attention. He glances my way, then down at the spot where the brunette sat, and raises a brow. He probably thought I was another creep hitting on one of his bar patrons.

A creep who for some reason called a stranger "Button." Why the fuck did I call her Button? Why not, sweetheart, or dear, or baby? I mean, I didn't call her baby because my sisters told me no woman wants to be mistaken for something helpless. But why *Button*?

I wasn't going to touch her either, but my fingertips were drawn to her waist like there was a magnet between us, and when I placed my lips against her cheek, there was the slightest hitch in her breath. So maybe that attraction went both ways?

But this protective instinct has backfired before—I seem to attract women who take advantage of my kindness. My sisters always warn me that I come on too strong and trust too easily. They said I'm like a lost puppy: following home the first pretty girl who looks my way.

But I didn't follow her. Instead, I stood there like an idiot after that guy left. I didn't even get her name.

"What will it be?" the bartender asks, finally stopping in front of me and flipping a bar towel over his shoulder.

"Bourbon, neat," I order and try to offer a friendly smile.

He sets a highball glass in front of me and pours with that casual accuracy bartenders have—that muscle memory to pour exactly two ounces while barely watching.

I take a sip of the amber liquid, letting its smoky flavor burn the back of my throat, hoping the drink will settle my nerves. This entire trip had me rattled. I had flown up here, spent all day in Eli's apartment, trying to convince him to show me some pages. Eli may have been a Pulitzer-winning author, but he hadn't written shit in over five years. And I couldn't sell something he wasn't writing.

"I've seen you in here before," the bartender says as he reorganizes bottles beneath the counter.

"Yeah," I say, leaning on the bar. "I'm in town for work a lot." Usually trying to convince Eli to put some words—any goddamn words—down on paper.

Eli has been my client for eight years. Six years since his debut literary novel, *The Gone Hours*, hit the *New York Times* bestseller list. By the end of that year, we were walking out of the Pulitzer luncheon with his name on a plaque and more offers than I could field in my inbox.

But then, a bad case of writer's block hit Eli when he started his second book. "Totally normal!" I told him, "It's not a big deal. Take a vacation, visit a monastery, sleep with beautiful women. Authors have all sorts of rituals to rediscover the muse." But Eli did none of those things. He moved into an apartment two blocks from this bar and has barely left since.

Now, I'm sitting on this stool, drinking bourbon and watching my own bank account dwindle. I have other clients, but no one like Eli. After you have one big success, people expect big things from you, and the pressure to deliver can be intense. Maybe Eli and I are more similar than I thought.

Bright pink lipstick smudges the edge of the abandoned glass next to mine. I pick it up and hold it to the light of the neon bar sign. The brunette was drinking bourbon, too. I smile. What else does she like?

Is she a morning person or a night owl?

Does she like her bacon crispy, or maybe she's a vegetarian?

I wonder what her go-to movie theater candy is—and suddenly I'm picturing us together in a dark theater, sharing a tub of popcorn and a box of Junior Mints.

"She's a good one," the bartender says, tipping his chin towards the glass I was holding. "Most would've made it worse. You didn't."

I set the glass down, feeling creepy for touching something she just held—like I'm some nut job. He's right. I could've made it worse—rescuing her from one creep just to turn around and hit on her myself. I need to snap out of it, stop daydreaming about strangers, and go upstairs to my hotel room.

Tomorrow, I plan to head back to Eli's and try to convince him to leave the house. If I can't get him to write, maybe I can at least get him to put some sun on his pale-ass skin. We could hit up the Japanese Tea Gardens or do something touristy like walking across the Golden Gate Bridge. I've never done that.

If the brunette's a local, I bet she's walked the bridge before. Maybe she could show me those secret cement slides I've heard about, hidden somewhere in the city.

Oh my god, Owen, go to bed, you freak.

Chapter 3

Liv

"Mom, I'm just not sure if I can make it tonight," I say, yawning and pulling my dark waves into a messy top knot.

"Don't tug on your hair like that, Olivia," my mother says, scowling at me over FaceTime. She's the only one who calls me Olivia—everyone else, even my dad, calls me Liv. "You'll give yourself split ends," she adds with a disapproving tut.

I'm not sure if that is true, but I let my hair drop to my shoulders and try to drag my fingers through the mess. I had finally slept, and by the looks of my hair and the pillow creases on my face, I had slept hard.

"You might benefit from a few highlights. Have you seen Ricardo lately?" My mother's hair is platinum blonde—thanks to Ricardo—and perfectly styled, even though it's barely 9 a.m. on a Saturday. Then again, Marlowe Arden has probably already played a round of tennis and is getting ready for brunch, while I'm just now dragging myself out of bed after too many bourbons and sleeping like the dead. "Maybe he can fit you in before the gala tonight."

"Work has been intense lately," I sigh and pour a cup of coffee from the machine on the counter. "I could really use the night to get ahead of the launch."

"Olivia, everyone will be there. You need to make an appearance, or people will think there is some rift between us."

I pause, struck by the irony of my mother bullying me into attending an event just so she can look like a good parent. But that's my mom—as long as everything *looks* perfect, she can pretend it actually is.

Andy's bedroom door opens, and she bounds out, looking way perkier than I feel. She is wearing her favorite cartoon-sushi-roll-covered pajama bottoms and a thin cami that leaves nothing to the imagination. But I had lived with her for the last three years and this was far from the first time I'd seen her boobs.

"Hey, Mrs. A!" Andy leans into FaceTime and waves at my mother, taking her own oversized coffee cup from the cabinet.

"Adeline," my mother replies coolly, "How's the glamorous world of leash-holding?"

"It's great," Andy says, spooning an ungodly amount of sugar into her coffee. "Better than chasing approval, Mrs. A." She puts a smacking kiss on my cheek, and my mother turns away from the screen like Andy had stuck her tongue in my mouth or worse, used off-brand skin care.

"Olivia," my mother continues. "Tonight is very important to your father. You need to take something seriously... for once."

I slip out of the apartment and into the hall. Andy has witnessed my mother's tirades more than once, and I want to spare her today's edition.

I shut the door. "I am taking something seriously. My job."

"Oh, Olivia, playing video games for a living is hardly taking things seriously."

I'm not going to respond. Despite my repeated attempts to explain my job to my mother, she consistently reduces it to "playing video games," "watching YouTube," or, her personal favorite, "wasting the expensive college degree they paid for."

My mother does not take the hint at my silence. "The gala starts at six; you need to be there by five thirty. What are you wearing? Not that yellow dress. That color does nothing for your complexion."

"Mom," I try to cut in, but she just pushes forward with her plans, disregarding anything I try to say...as usual.

"You know what? I can't trust you to be on time. I'm going to have Peter pick you up. It makes more sense for you to show up together, anyway."

What?

"Please tell me you didn't tell Peter I was going to the gala."

"Of course not. I did better. I told him you needed a date for the gala."

"Mom!"

"What? Lord knows you would not bring a date on your own. I don't know why you are being so difficult about Peter."

"I don't like Peter, and honestly, I don't even think he likes me. You and Dad have to stop this obsession."

"Nonsense, what does liking someone have to do with getting married?"

"Married? What are you talking about?"

I hear footsteps on the stairs out the front door, and I tuck in closer to my apartment door. I don't need Cal, my upstairs neighbor, or that slightly scary woman from 2B, to overhear this conversation.

"Olivia, you aren't getting any younger," she huffs. "I'm done having this conversation. Peter will pick you up at five thirty and don't wear yellow."

"Mom!" I shout back into the phone. "I'm not going to the gala with Peter!"

The front door opens, only it's not Cal who enters the lobby carrying a drink tray with two coffee cups. It's a man with dark hair and jeans that hug his thighs in a way that makes it impossible not to notice the muscle beneath. Something about him is so familiar that I do a double-take. Those piercing green eyes.

"Button?" he asks, coming to an abrupt stop near the mailboxes.

"Why on earth not?" my mother's voice trills through the lobby. She dislikes being contradicted.

"Because I am already bringing someone." The words tumble out of my mouth before I register what I'm saying.

The stranger meets my stare, but I don't miss the way his gaze flicks down my body before returning to my face—or the way he drags his bottom lip between his teeth. Then, he looks away with the same sweet blush across his cheeks as last night.

"You are?" my mother says incredulously. "Who?"

"My fiancé."

Chapter 4

Owen

She's even more stunning than last night.

Dark waves, tousled and spilling over one shoulder of an oversized, gray sweatshirt that nearly swallows the tiny, hot pink shorts. Her long, tanned legs stretch down to bare feet, toes painted a glossy, unapologetic red. She looks effortless, like the kind of woman who doesn't know she's the most captivating person in the room.

She jams her finger against her phone screen, silencing whoever she is talking to. "What are you doing here?" She stands up a little taller, her nerves evident.

"I didn't follow you!" I say, which is exactly what someone who is following her would say. "I'm just..." I gesture toward the stairs, "visiting someone in the building. Do you live here?"

"I'm not telling you that."

"Of course," I hold up my hand and the coffees I'm juggling in concession. "I'm Owen."

"Why did you call me Button?"

I let out a self-deprecating laugh. "Honestly, I have no idea." I shake my head, feeling the heat flush across my cheeks.

"You blush a lot," she muses, but I catch a faint smile.

"Yeah," I nod, "my sisters called me Pink for an entire summer."

"Who are you visiting?" she asks, looking up the stairs.

"Um...Eli..." I hesitate. Eli's last name is Patterson, but he writes under the pen name Elijah Thorne. He isn't very social, and I'm not sure what the other tenants in the building know about him or which name would sound more believable. "3A?" I offer, but my voice tips up in the end, like I'm questioning my facts.

She nods. "I see him at the mailbox occasionally." Her eyes flit to her closed door before she takes a step towards me and holds out her hand. "I'm Liv," she says, "Olivia, but please call me Liv."

"Owen," I shift the coffee carrier and take her outstretched hand.

"You said that already," she chuckles, and it's like a little bell trilling. My feet take a few steps toward her on their own volition.

"Yeah, I guess I did."

"Okay, Owen, it's nice to officially meet you." She turns back toward her door.

"Who were you talking to?" I'm not sure why I ask, but she looked upset.

Liv bites her lip, and I have to fight the urge to reach out and free it with my thumb. "My mother."

"Ahh, I get it," I say. "I have one of those, too."

"The kind who's always meddling in your life and trying to set you up with your dad's business partner's son to secure their seafood empire legacy?" Liv says with a heavy exhale.

"Well," I chuckle slightly, "Not exactly, but my mother and two older sisters enjoy sticking their noses into my business like it's their job. But it's because they love us, right?"

She just huffs.

"So, this seafood heir..." I ask. "Is your fiancé?" And I don't know why my heart pinches a little.

"No, I think I meant you actually," she winces. "Sorry. My mom wants me to go to this stupid gala, and I just wanted her to back off, and I was surprised to see you in the lobby, and last night you pretended to be my husband to get that guy to leave me alone and..." She takes a big inhale. "I just blurted out that you were my fiancé."

"Me?" I ask, surprised, but the word "fiancé" on her lips sends an embarrassing jolt to my groin.

"Sorry about that. I didn't mean to drag you into my family drama." She scrunches her nose in a way that is wildly adorable, and I wonder if that's where my involuntary Button nickname came from.

"I'll go."

"What?"

"I'll go," I shift towards her. "You told your mother you were bringing your fiancé, and I'm free tonight, so I'll go."

"No," she says. "I don't even know you, and I wouldn't subject my worst enemy to an evening with my mother, much less a stranger."

The door behind her opens, and a petite blonde, sporting a sky-high ponytail and oversized headphones, skips into the lobby. "Hey, Lollipop, I'm going to pick up the boys. I'll see you later." She spots me standing just a few feet from her friend, and a wide smile spreads across her face. "Heeeyyy," she says, "Who's this?"

"Andy, this is Owen. He's visiting that guy upstairs. Owen, this is my roommate, Andy."

"The old guy or the recluse?" Andy whispers to Liv, but she's loud enough for me to hear.

"The recluse," she whispers back, and I can't help but laugh. I'm going to give Eli so much shit later when I tell him the other people in his building think he's a shut-in.

Andy nods, as if that explains something, before digging a pink lip gloss out of her pocket and smearing it on her lips.

"Well, he's cute," she says matter-of-factly before bounding out the door.

I watch her roommate exit the building. When I turn back, Liv is watching me.

"Why would you offer to go to the gala with me tonight? Is this some ploy to get in my pants?"

"What!" My voice clicks up an octave, and I can tell by the heat spreading across my collar and the smirk on Liv's face that my face has turned beet red. "Not at all! I just..." I shrug, "...wanted to help."

"Why?"

"I don't know. My parents always taught us that if someone needs something and you can help, you do. You need a date, and...I'm available."

"Your girlfriend won't mind?"

"No girlfriend to mind."

Liv sighs again. "Fine, you're right. I don't want to face my mother alone tonight. Maybe a fake fiancé buys me enough time to survive this launch at work, and in a few weeks, I can tell her we broke up. One more way I can disappoint her."

I deflate a little hearing Liv say we will break up, but I just smile and nod. "Happy to help."

"Alright then, Owen, from fake husband to fake fiancé. Let's do this."

Chapter 5

Liv

"Okay, then...great," Owen says. His tongue darts out to moisten his lip, and I can't help but track its movement. "What time should I pick you up?"

"You don't have to do that. We can just meet there," I say, trying to regain my composure.

"No way, this may be a fake date, but my sisters would kill me if they found out I wasn't a real gentleman."

"Alright," I laugh, "Pick me up at six, wear the suit you wore last night." I catch Owen's eyes flick to my body, and I realize I'm still in my pajamas, while Owen is dressed in dark jeans and a fitted dark sweater. "I promise to be in a dress."

Something about the faint color tinging Owen's cheeks again causes a flutter behind my ribs. "And...thanks for doing this."

"It will be fun," Owen says. "I'm pretty good at selling a story."

"Oh, right, the story." I shift to lean against my door. "We should probably know some basic information about each other to make tonight a little more believable?"

"Do you..." He gestures to the coffees he's still holding. "Want a coffee?"

"Oh my god! You were taking coffee to your friend when I sidelined you. I'm so sorry."

"It's no problem. He's fine alone," he says, laughing, and points to each one. "I have an oat milk latte and an Americano."

"Oh, oat milk lattes are my favorite."

"Mine too," he smiles, and his eyes crinkle a little at the corners. I try to place his age—he seems around mine, in his early thirties. His dark hair looks freshly trimmed but is a little long on top in an effortlessly messy way. It's the kind of hair you want to run your fingers through.

"Oh, then that one was yours? You should have it."

He holds the latte cup out to me. "Please, take it."

I take the offered cup and consider inviting him inside. Something about Owen makes me feel instantly comfortable, just like last night when he kissed my temple. For some reason, it didn't feel awkward at all. Now, his presence settles my nerves, the ones my mother fried earlier.

"Want to sit outside?" Owen gestures to the front door.

Yes, that is a better idea.

He holds the door for me, and I settle on the rock wall around our unit's small front garden. It's a beautiful day, with no fog and only a gentle breeze.

"Okay, so what do we need to know to make this whole fake fiancé thing believable?" I take a sip of the coffee. It's gone a little cold, but the creamy coffee is still delicious.

"Um, what is your last name?"

"Arden."

"Olivia Arden, but you prefer Liv," his lip tips up. "I'm Owen Bishop. Where did we meet?"

"Um, let's keep things as close to the truth as possible, so in a bar?" I ask. "And you have two older sisters who live...where?"

"In Ohio, where I grew up. My parents, two sisters, their husbands, and my combined five nieces and nephews still live there."

"But not you?"

"I live in Santa Barbara now."

"I love Santa Barbara! Julia Child's favorite Mexican restaurant is there."

"Yeah, La Super Rica," he confirms.

"Their chorizo quesadilla is my favorite." I shift on the rock wall so I'm facing Owen a little more directly.

"That lady, hand-making tortillas in the back? Can't beat them."

I let out a little sigh. The sun, the coffee, the delightful conversation: This fact-finding mission for our fake date is more enjoyable than most real first dates I've been on—not that there have been many lately. "And what do you do in Santa Barbara?"

"I'm a literary agent."

"Ahh," I laugh. "So when you said you could sell a story, you were being literal?"

"It's a bad industry joke," he scrunches his nose, and there's something about him that's so endearing, it's disarming.

"I work for an agency based in LA," he goes on. "But I work from home."

"Me too, most of the time anyway. I'm a UX director for a wellness start-up."

His lip quirks up a little, and my hackles go up.

"What?"

"Nothing. You said your mom wasn't impressed with your job. Being a UX director for a start-up sounds pretty impressive to me."

"You're not Marlowe Arden; nothing impresses her, least of all me."

Owen studies me for a moment, but doesn't press at my last comment. "So your mom is Marlowe, and your dad?"

"Salvator, but everyone calls him Big Sal."

"Big Sal? Should I be nervous?"

"Maybe a little?" I shrug, but Owen looks more than a little nervous. "He's harmless. He'll hardly talk to us, anyway."

"Do you have any siblings?" Owen asks. He shifts his body to face me, bringing our knees only inches apart.

"An older brother, Spenser. But he wants nothing to do with my dad's restaurant chains or, honestly, my parents at all, so that's why they are so hell-bent on marrying me off to Peter. Spenser lives in Puerto Escondido and teaches surfing to tourists."

"But your parents don't find your job impressive?"

I press my lips together, unsure how to explain my family's complicated dynamic. "Okay, but how did we go from meeting in a bar to being engaged, especially if you don't live here?"

"Well," he scrunches his nose in concentration. "I'm in San Francisco a lot for work. Maybe I started coming more often to see you." The faint flush that appears on his cheeks is so...sweet that I find myself leaning slightly closer before I catch myself.

"Let's just keep it simple," I say, clearing my throat and easing back. "You were in town on an extended work trip, and we met at a bar. We ended up seeing a lot of each other after that. It just felt easy. A few weeks later, you took me on a picnic at Ocean Beach, my favorite beach, and...you asked. And I said yes."

"That's it? That's all I did to woo you?"

"It will be fine. Marlowe and Sal won't talk to us long enough to get any more backstory."

Just then, Andy comes through the gate with three enormous dogs, all pulling and lunging in different directions. Andy looks completely unbothered by her charges' energy, but her eyes go wide when she sees Owen and me with our coffee cups.

"Um, Ladybug?" she says, shifting the leashes to her other hand. "I forgot my phone inside. Can you help me find it?"

She thrusts the trio of leashes towards Owen. "Can you hold the boys for me?"

"Um...sure?" Owen sounds unsure but takes the massive dogs' leather leads.

"Andy?" I ask, but she grabs my elbow and steers me toward the building.

"We'll just be a minute!" she calls over her shoulder before pushing me through the front door.

"I know for a fact your phone is permanently attached to your palm," I say the minute Andy closes our apartment door, "so what do you need to say?"

"Uh...what's going on out there, Liberty Bell?" Andy asks, lacing her fingers together under her chin.

"What do you mean?"

"You appear to be having coffee with a man in our garden. An extremely hot man at that. The same man I saw in our lobby over thirty-six minutes ago when I left to pick up the boys. Correct me if I'm wrong, but I think this now qualifies as your longest relationship in at least a year."

"Andy!" I scold, but she's not wrong. "RootDown has taken up a lot of my time. Owen is just a guy I met, and he agreed to pretend we're engaged for my mother's gala tonight."

"Hum..." Andy twirls her ponytail. "Why not just say he's a guy you met...why fake date? Why not take him to the gala as your real date?"

"Because I just met him."

"Oh right, that makes sense..." Andy says sarcastically.

"My mom thinks she's going to convince me to marry Peter tonight."

"Your dad's fish sticks have a better personality than that dude," Andy agrees.

"Exactly. So this just feels cleaner. A clear agreement, no messy feelings."

"Lily Pad, I know that asshole Isaac messed you up, but feelings are not the enemy here, no matter how emotionally undermining he was."

"It wasn't..." I stop myself before finishing with *that bad*, because it was. My ex, Isaac, had a talent for pointing out all my flaws—sometimes subtle, sometimes not—and then acting like I should thank him for sticking around. Like I was supposed to be grateful he was willing to 'fix' me every time I fell short. But in the end, even he decided I was too high-maintenance to fix.

"This is not about him," I dismiss her concern. "This is about getting my mother off my back for a night."

"Maybe, but fake dating a guy who clearly makes your stomach do that *fluttery thing*—that's a move made by someone who's scared to let herself have a good time."

"He does not make my stomach do...whatever...anything. It's fake. That's all we agreed to. That's all I want." Andy didn't respond. She just gave me a stupid, knowing look. "Now go get your dogs back from my fake fiancé."

"Just be sure I'm on the guest list for your fake wedding," Andy says, pulling me into a tight hug, her bubble gum scent filling the air between us. "You're allowed to enjoy this, Liv, even if it's a little messy."

Chapter 6

Owen

I miraculously find street parking directly in front of Liv's apartment ten minutes before six. And I had to actively try not to arrive any earlier.

After Liv and I said goodbye this morning, I went upstairs to see Eli. We talked for a while about writing, but when it became clear that he didn't want to discuss his non-progress, I tried to convince him to come with me into the City for the afternoon. After yesterday's strange rainfall, today was lovely.

Despite what Andy had said earlier, Eli wasn't a complete shut-in. He goes to the gym every day, wearing noise-canceling headphones and talking to no one. Even though his entire diet consists of only five items, he procures them himself. Occasionally, he visits the planetarium in Golden Gate Park. The stars, he says, reminded him that there's a bigger world out there, even if he didn't always want to be part of it. But I was worried about him.

He shut down my idea of Chinatown dumplings, but I left with a promise—or maybe a threat—to return tomorrow.

I had been buzzing all day to get back here. Despite knowing it was a fake date to placate her mother, my time with Liv in the garden earlier was the most enjoyable date I'd had in months. She was charming, funny, and probably the

smartest person I'd ever met. And that was saying something, since I represented two senators, a global humanitar-
ian, and a Pulitzer Prize-winning author—even if the latter
wouldn't leave his apartment. I couldn't believe Liv needed
someone to pretend to be her date. That men weren't banging down her door to date her for real.

"Yes?" Her voice cracks through the speaker, and it is still
the most beautiful sound I've ever heard.

"It's Owen."

The door clicks, and I enter the building. I'm about to
knock on 1B when a tall man jogs down the stairs in running
clothes.

"Hey, man," he gives a cliché dude-chin-tip, but I catch the
way he slows to watch me, his eyes flicking to the bouquet in
my hand. "You here for Andy?"

"Um, Liv, actually."

"Really? Good for her. I'm Cal," he says, holding out his
hand. "I live upstairs. I've seen you here before, though?"

"Oh, yeah, I'm friends with Eli...in 3A," I offer.

"Right, sure. How's he doing?"

"Fine." I don't want to make small talk with this guy. I
want to see Liv.

"Sorry," Cal ducks his head. "I've lived in this building for
a long time. I guess I kind of look out for everyone. Anyway,
enjoy your evening. Tell Liv I said hello."

A strange taste coats my throat bitter and acrid like jeal-
ousy. I know I will not tell her that her neighbor, who looks
like a taller Hemsworth brother, said hello.

Just as I raise my hand to knock, the door swings open. I
open and close my mouth a few times, like a stupid guppy,
at all that is Liv Arden in front of me.

"Hey, Owen," she says, and I can't form words. Her dark
hair, untamed this morning, now falls in elegant curls over
the shoulders of her deep wine dress. It has a high collar, long
sleeves, and stops just below her knees, but it's the damned

sexiest dress I've ever seen. "Thanks for coming," she adds when I still don't reply. "I wasn't sure if you'd go through with it."

"Of course," I stammer. I can hardly tear my eyes away from the way the dress hugs her every curve. "I promised I would."

"Right." Her voice clipped, and I'm not sure what I said, probably because I was gawking at her like a psychopath. "Should we go?"

"These are for you," I say, regaining enough composure to hand her the pale pink peonies.

"These are my favorite." She looks stunned. "But you didn't have to. This isn't a real date."

Right.

I smile at her, but I feel like an idiot. This is not a date. She is not my girlfriend, and she certainly isn't my fiancée. *Shit.*

"Then you're going to hate the next thing I brought you," I say, reaching into my pocket and pulling out a small box.

"Owen." She says with a rush of air when I open the ring box.

"It's nothing, it's from Chinatown," I backpedal. "I thought it would help the story." But now I'm kicking myself for doing something so stupid.

"It's perfect," she laughs. The laugh I'm already starting to crave. She holds out her left hand, and I slide the round, brilliant-cut cubic zirconia onto her finger. My throat goes dry at the sight of that nineteen-dollar ring resting there like it belongs.

"Alright," she sighs, "Let's get this over with."

Right, I scold myself again; this is a fake date. *Get it together and act like you're faking it.* She ducks back inside her apartment to leave the flowers, and when she returns, I offer her my arm. "Shall we, dear?"

"Aw," she glances up at me, taking my elbow, "I kinda like Button."

Chapter 7

Liv

This is a terrible idea.

I tighten my grip on Owen's elbow, and he reaches around to place a comforting hand on top of mine. He's good at this fake fiancé thing already.

My parents' yacht club exudes old money and generational privilege. The guest list comprises a who's who of Bay Area elites, all dressed in sleek suits and luxurious fabrics, with the sort of 'natural' beauty that requires a team of specialists to maintain.

Owen takes a glass of champagne from a passing waiter and hands it to me before taking one for himself. Either he senses I need it, or he requires the liquid to resolve himself as well. I hope he isn't already regretting his decision.

"Ready for this?" I ask under my breath.

"As I'll ever be." He clinks his glass with mine, and we both take a long sip.

"Good, because my mother is coming this way."

"Olivia!" my mother coos with her *we're-in-public-and-I-love-my-daughter-so-much* voice. "There you are!"

"Mom." I let her air kiss me on both cheeks, then smooth my hair, inspecting me like I'm a prize horse.

"Owen, dear! It's so good to see you," she pulls Owen into a dramatic hug. After I hung up on her this morning, she texted saying it was an absolute embarrassment that she didn't know I was engaged, and she at least needed to know his name so as not to tip off her friends to the fact that she was being 'kept in the dark' about her daughter's love life.

Owen, for his part, didn't miss a beat. "It's great to see you, Mrs. Arden. You look lovely tonight."

"Oh, stop, I've told you to call me Marlowe," she says, glancing around, and I roll my eyes.

A waiter passes, and I reach for whatever fried blob of something is perched on a tasting spoon on his tray.

"Olivia," my mother snaps under her breath, shaking her head once in disapproval. I drop my hand. Owen, who had also reached for an appetizer, pulls his hand back when he sees I didn't take one.

"Coco," she calls out to a woman passing, "have you met my future son-in-law? He's a literary agent." She presents Owen to the woman who has the collective scent of wealth, white wine, and high-end filler.

"Hello." Coco holds out her hand like a limp fish for Owen. "A literary agent? Anyone we've heard of?" But she says it with an air of 'prove yourself,' not curiosity.

I hold my breath. I have no idea who Owen represents.

"Well," Owen smiles at the woman, "I just secured an offer for Senator Meredith Langford's memoir." He reaches out and lets his hand rest at the base of my spine, and my heart flutters a little. "And I represent Elijah Thorne."

"You do?" I whisper, impressed.

"Oh, my book club read *The Gone Hours*—hauntingly beautiful," Coco says. She looks surprised, or at least I think she does, the filler doesn't leave much room for nuance.

"Thank you, I'll tell him you said so. I'm seeing him this week." His eyes dart down to me, seeking approval, and I nod my head a little. He is really good at this taming rich white women thing.

"Now," my mother stops Coco, who is trying to leave, with a hand on her arm, "you have to hear their adorable engagement story. Sal and I were just beside ourselves."

"Mom," I murmur under my breath. While I had told my mom Owen's name and profession, all I included in our text exchange was that we got engaged at Ocean Beach a few weeks ago, hardly adorable. My stomach turns. Can we pull this off?

Owen is quiet for a moment, and I worry he's panicking or chickening out and about to blow our cover when he reaches down and laces our hands together instead.

"Mrs. Arden, you know I think your daughter is incredible," he starts, but then he brings our joined hands to his mouth and gently kisses my Chinatown ring. A low heat curls in my belly. "We met at a bar near her apartment. I was in town visiting Elijah. But then one conversation turned into five hours, followed by a late-night run to her favorite taqueria for chorizo quesadillas. I extended my stay, and we started seeing each other every chance we got—museum dates, roller-skating in Golden Gate Park, and a disastrous attempt at a pottery class." He looks down at me and smiles, like we shared this non-existent memory, before continuing. "Somewhere between an impassioned argument that Lara Croft deserved better writing and burning pancakes in her kitchen, I knew. I realize it was sudden, but I think I knew she was the one that first night we met at the bar. I think she is the most fascinating person I've ever known, and I couldn't imagine my world without her in it. So, on one long weekend visit, I took her to Ocean Beach, her favorite spot, at sunset. I brought her favorite dumplings from the place in Chinatown she loves, and I asked her to marry me. She said yes, or, actually, she laughed so hard she cried, but then she said yes."

I stare at Owen, my jaw slack, and watch the familiar blush crawl across his cheeks. He tries to loosen the grip he has on our hands, but I hold tight. He turns to look at me with something like an apology in his eyes, but I don't want him to apologize.

I tug our joined hands toward me and lean in, placing a delicate kiss on his lips. A little whoosh escapes the back of his throat, and his other hand comes around to tangle in my hair. I try to deepen the kiss, but my mother clears her throat beside us, and we both pull away. Owen looks a little breathless, like he's just run a mile. I feel a little...well, I'm not sure what I feel.

"Isn't that the sweetest?" my mother says, but I can tell she's a little taken aback, too. "We are, of course, going to throw a big party for these two lovebirds, but you know how it is, Coco. I had to get through this gala first. I told Sal that I simply couldn't plan two parties at once, no matter how much I wanted to. Keep an eye out for the invitation!"

"Of course," Coco just nods an odd, frozen smile and walks away.

"Ugh, that woman," my mother sighs as soon as Coco is out of earshot, then turns toward Owen. After I flung myself at him, he took a small step back, no longer touching me. I can't believe I kissed him. He did not sign up for that. "Now, Owen, dear, Olivia said you were a literary agent, but I had no idea you represented Elijah Thorne. A Pulitzer! Impressive."

"He was my first client. We both got lucky with each other," Owen says, regaining his composure. I, on the other hand, still feel a little dizzy from our fake kiss. After all, he was just going along with it to sell our story.

"Hum, at least one of you has a proper job," my mother says, throwing up her hands. "Olivia, you're lucky you found someone willing to put up with your erratic work prospects."

"Mom, can we not?"

"What? I'm just saying. You don't have the most stable track recorded. You are a bit of a risk, dear."

I let out a shaky breath and want to pull Owen away before my mother can say anything else.

"I hope you'll beg my pardon, Mrs. Arden," Owen clears his throat, and reaches out to take my hand again, "but I'm not sure you're clear on what Liv does for a living."

"I am very clear that Olivia quit a successful career with a major tech company—one that her father pulled all sorts of strings at to even get her an interview." All the warmth my mother had been showering Owen with drained from her face. This was the Marlowe Arden I knew. "Not to mention wasting the extremely pricey degree that we paid for, so she could spend her days tracking strangers' moods with emojis. So yes, Mr. Bishop, I'm quite clear on what my daughter does, or rather, what she doesn't do for a living. She might have you enamored, but be careful—Olivia's always been a lot of work and when things get tough, she tends to move on."

I feel like I've had my knees knocked out from under me. My mother can be direct, even mean, but this feels like a low blow—even for her. I'm used to her undermining my career or criticizing my fashion choices, but I don't know why it hurts so much to hear her insinuate I might 'move on' from Owen. Yes, he's technically my fake fiancé, but she doesn't know that. And Isaac left me! But maybe it was my fault—maybe I am too much work. Maybe I do always fall a little short.

I let my hand fall from Owen's grip; this wasn't fair to him. He signed up to wear a suit, eat some tuna tartare, and pretend he's known me for more than twelve hours. But as soon as our hands part, he reaches around my waist and tugs me to his side, his fingers digging protectively into my hip.

"Liv's company, RootDown, is the fastest-growing start-up in the wellness space, with over 800,000 members, and is on track to triple its valuation in the next five years. She led the design overhaul that improved member retention by nearly fifty percent." He looks down and kisses the top of my head. "She was also recognized with the Ada Lovelace Award for Innovation in Human-Computer Interaction—something only a handful of people in her field have achieved, and no one at her age. So you're right; she has me enamored because she's badass. But also, because I respect her, and it's a bit shortsighted not to give her the credit she deserves."

My mother's eyes go wide, but I hardly notice because I'm staring at Owen. No one, and I mean no one, has ever defended me to my mother. Spenser tried when we both lived at home, but he always backed down when my mother's claws came out. I do not know how Owen figured all that out about me, but it sends a warm surge through my body. Owen's hand is still digging into my hip, and he hasn't broken his stare with my mother. I slide my hand around his waist, under his suit jacket, and turn into his chest. He looks down at me and strums his thumb over the ruching on the side of my dress, his breathing elevated.

"Do you want to get out of here?" I whisper.

He nods, "Yeah, Button, I do."

Chapter 8

Owen

"Liv, I'm so sorry," I whisper as soon as the valet disappears to get my car. She doesn't say a word, but she doesn't let go of my hand either—still clutching it like she has since we walked out of the ballroom. I remind myself it's just part of the act, a performance until we're out of sight of her parents and their curious friends.

I can't believe I spoke to her mother like that. But that same instinct I felt in the bar last night—that primal need to protect her—came rushing back the moment Marlowe Arden started picking her apart. From the way she wore her hair—those gorgeous, soft curls she called "messy." To what she ate—I thought she might actually slap Liv's hand. To her career, which, from what I learned earlier, thanks to a deep dive on Google, is nothing short of exceptional.

My rental car appears over the rise of the driveway, and I wait while the valet holds the door open for Liv as she tucks her dress inside. After tipping the guy, I hurry around to the driver's side. I glance at Liv, but she's just staring straight ahead. I'm ready to beg for forgiveness, call her an Uber, or even go back inside and apologize to her parents—whatever it takes to get her to talk to me again.

"I'm starving," she says, turning to flash me a wry smile, like I hadn't just insulted her mother within minutes of meeting her. "Want to go get pizza in North Beach?"

"Um..." I stammer, "Yeah, I do." And I ease the car out of the yacht club parking lot and head across town.

"How did you know all that about me?" she asks as we walk away from the late-night pizza stand. She's balancing a slice of pepperoni on a plate and wearing my suit jacket. I like the way it looks on her.

I take a bite of my slice before shrugging, "Google?" The fact was, I spent so much time looking her up online this afternoon that I felt like a creepy stalker.

"Why?" She stops in the middle of the sidewalk, and I worry that she also thinks I'm a creepy stalker. But the look in her eyes—something like hope and maybe gratitude—allows me to answer.

"I guess I wanted to make sure I was prepared for tonight. Before meeting a potential client, I do as much research as I can to make sure I come across as interested and well-informed. I was meeting your parents and people who would obviously know the specifics of your life."

Liv nods, but the light in her eyes fades just a little. Her smile doesn't quite reach the corners of her mouth. I clear my throat, suddenly unsure. "But I also meant what I said to your mother." I glance at her, trying to read her face. "You're...you're the most fascinating person I think I've ever met."

"Your newest client, Senator Langford, was raised in a cult, practically kidnapped her three younger siblings to raise them herself, and now she's the Democrats' best shot at the White House," she counters.

"Like I said, you're the most fascinating person I've ever met," I say, taking a bite of my pizza to keep from saying too much. Liv seems content with that, and we fall into step again.

"Is the Eli you were visiting in my apartment Elijah Thorne?" she asks when we reach what looks like an abandoned lot turned parklet—string lights stretch between two buildings, casting a soft glow over benches and picnic tables.

"Yeah, he uses a pen name." I nod towards a small table in the space. It's buzzing with people eating pizza or ice cream, couples leaning close on benches, families enjoying the rare warm evening.

"Huh," she muses, taking a seat. "A Pulitzer winner in my building. I thought he was some weirdo holed up in there doing Nigerian prince scams or in the witness protection program."

I let out a genuine laugh. "Eli is complicated." I take a sip of my soda. I rarely share details about my clients' lives, but then again, I never offer to fake date a stranger either. However, something about Liv—the way she carries herself and the little sly glint behind her eyes—makes me want to tell her everything. Hell, she could probably get me to believe she was a Nigerian prince. "Eli had a rough childhood, and then success came fast. I think he hasn't figured out how to reconcile the two."

"Who you thought you were and who you end up being?" Liv says. And I nod. "I get that."

"He just needs someone who believes in him. I want to be that for him," I say.

"Well, I'll be nicer to him at the mailbox now that I know he's not some creepy dude watching internet porn from his penthouse."

I almost choke on my soda with a surprised laugh, and it pulls a smile from Liv. Suddenly, all I can think about is how to make her do it again.

We watch the delightful chaos in front of us for a few moments—kids darting across a makeshift stage at the back of the lot, dogs sniffing each other, people laughing loudly. Liv pulls my jacket tighter around her shoulders and leans into me, slightly, almost without realizing it. For a second, I almost wish her mother were here to give me an excuse to slip my arm around her.

"So your mom." I begin cautiously. "Is she always..."

"A total bitch? Yeah, pretty much." Liv answers, popping the last of her pizza crust into her mouth.

"I was going to say, 'that intense.'"

Liv lets out a long sigh, and I'm instantly sorry I brought up her mom.

"You know what you said in my lobby earlier about our families getting in our business because they love us? I think that's what my mom believes she's doing." She stops talking, and I think that's all I'm going to get of the Marlowe Adren story, but then Liv turns on the bench to face me directly, her eyes momentarily searching my face, maybe for permission. I fight the urge again to touch her.

"I think I've never truly lived up to my parents' expectations of me," she continues. "Like I'm never quite enough. No matter how many things I do right, my mom finds some way that I let her down."

"Everything you've done in your career? It's not enough for her?" I ask, not sure if I'm out of line.

"Oh, my career is a huge thing. Like, as a kid, I was *obsessed* with video games—totally in love with them. But my parents flat-out refused to let me have any kind of gaming console." She glances up at me. "That's actually how I got into computers. I had one, but I wasn't allowed to download anything fun, so I...taught myself how to code my own games."

"See, I was right, totally badass," I tell her, and that earns me another smile.

"So after high school, I thought if I went to a top school, got perfect grades, became some kind of tech powerhouse, they'd *have* to respect it, you know? But they still dismissed it. Said I majored in video games and weed." She shook her head. "I've never even smoked pot, Owen. It's like it was never enough or the *right* enough for them."

"But your brother's a surf instructor?" My head tips to the side, studying her. "I mean, that sounds pretty badass too. Does he get the same third degree?"

Liv shrugs. "Maybe at first. But he's never cared about pleasing them, so they stopped trying somewhere around high school. He's only two years older than me, but they figured out pretty quickly I was the more...pliable one. Easier to mold. So they just let him go and focused on me instead. Honestly? I'm jealous."

"If they only love the version of you they can control...then they're missing the best parts."

She glances at me, surprised, like she wasn't expecting anyone to say it out loud. Her fingers fidget with the cuff of my jacket around her shoulders before she gives the faintest shake of her head and looks away. But there's something softer in her expression now, and I hope she heard me, anyway.

"Ice cream?" I say, changing the subject, and point at the little cart in the courtyard.

Liv smiles and stands.

"Sit," I encourage. "I'll bring it to you. What flavor?"

"Cookies and cream."

"My favorite, too," I say, barely above a whisper.

I return with two bowls, and we both take a few bites before she speaks again.

"Tonight," she goes on, softer now, but like she wants to, "she specifically told me not to wear yellow. So, of course, I wore this dress," she says, gesturing to herself. "Because apparently, I should only wear jewel tones."

"Wait, your mom told you not to wear yellow?" My blood pressure rises.

"Yeah. She says it washes me out." She rolls her eyes. "Then she didn't even mention the dress—just said I should've worn my hair up."

"For the record, that dress is incredible on you," I say. "And you wore that yellow top last night, right? I didn't notice any washing out."

Her eyes narrow slightly. "You remember what I was wearing last night?"

I want to tell her I not only remember the shirt she was wearing—a pale yellow blouse with billowy sleeves, still speckled from the rain she'd been caught in, thin enough that I could see the ridge of her collarbone and the faint outline of her bra through the fabric. That I'd noticed how she smelled when I got close—marshmallows and honey-suckle, with a hint of the bourbon she'd been sipping. I want her to know I'd clocked the way she nervously tapped her middle finger on the bar when that guy wouldn't leave her alone. But mostly, I remember how her breath hitched—just slightly—when I leaned in to kiss her.

"My sisters are eleven months apart and eight years older than me," I say instead. "They are best friends, and I was their living doll from the day my parents brought me home from the hospital. I've worn more dresses in my life than you probably have."

Liv lets out a laugh that I want to bottle.

"Your family sounds great. Like they're busybodies, but they actually care." And there is a little sadness behind Liv's eyes.

"Yeah, they do." Sometimes a little too much.

My phone blasts out the chorus to "We Are Family," and I quickly silence it. "Speak of the twin devils...that's my sisters' ringtone," I say by way of explanation.

"You can take it if you need to," Liv says, putting a spoonful of her cookies and cream into her mouth in a way that makes me jealous of the spoon.

"No," I roll my eyes playfully, "they will never let me off the phone, and especially if they know I'm still with you."

"You told your sisters about this?" Liv asks, a note of concern in her voice.

"I told them I was helping a friend who needed a plus one tonight," I say, keeping it simple.

She leans in. "What did they say?"

"They said it was very on brand for me," I reply with a small smile, taking another bite of my ice cream. I don't mention their warning about coming on too strong and scaring her off.

Liv chuckles softly. "I get it. You strike me as the 'save-the-day' kind of guy."

"You're staying at the Whitmore?"

My eyes dart to hers and my dick responds embarrassingly to her asking which hotel I'm staying at.

"Um, yeah." I try to shift subtly in my car seat at the image of her in my hotel room. Those brown curls fanning out over my pillow, her creamy skin naked, tangled in the white sheets, her cheeks flushed from—*oh my god, Owen, get it together*. I clear my throat. "It's nice, understated, close to Eli."

"It's next door to Bar None. That explains why you were there last night."

"Yeah," my voice comes out in a little squeak. She looks over, and the streetlight casts a beautiful glow across her skin. She is radiant.

"So you have a parking spot there? At the Whitmore?"

My breath hitches a little, and I just nod.

"Want to park and grab a drink?"

I nod again and try to swallow the lump growing in my throat.

"Then I'm only two blocks away. I can walk home."

My hope and my dick deflate and that lump in my throat turns into a stone in my stomach. But I snap out of it. I did her a favor; we're fake dating for one night, and that's over. We had a nice time getting a slice of pizza, and now we're going to grab one drink before we go our separate ways with a handshake and nothing more.

An hour later, after we've nursed our bourbons for as long as we realistically can, I still don't want the night to end. "Can I walk you home?"

"Oh, you don't need to do that. I walk home from Bar None all the time."

I should agree. I should say goodnight, shake her hand, and head upstairs to my hotel room.

"But your sisters would be disappointed in you if you didn't walk a lady home?" she continues, raising an eyebrow in a mocking smirk.

"Very disappointed," I confirm as solemnly as I can while my heart hammers around my chest like a *Looney Tunes* character.

"Let's go then," she says with a smile, and I toss a few twenties on the bar—completely unconcerned with the change. I follow her out the door, the same one I'd stared at last night, wishing I'd had the nerve to chase after her then.

God—was it only last night that I met this beautiful stranger? It feels like I've known Liv my whole life.

It's cooled off when we step out of the bar, the quintessential San Francisco fog having slid back into Liv's neighborhood. She's still wearing my jacket, and I want to climb back inside it with her still in it.

We make small talk until her building appears, the two blocks feeling like two steps. I watch her punch her code into the keypad. I'm not sure if I should leave her here or walk her all the way to her apartment door, but she holds the glass door for me, so I follow her inside.

"Owen," she says, turning to face me when we reach her door, "I never thought I would be thanking someone for being my fake fiancé, but once again, Thank you for pretending to be in love with me to get me out of a yet another compromising situation."

She bites her lip, and before I can stop myself, my hand cups her jaw. Her brown eyes widen, and I catch the subtle quickening of her breath, the way her pupils darken at my touch. I pause, waiting, when she leans in just slightly.

"I know we've been pretending tonight," I say softly, "but I'd like to kiss you for real. Would that be okay?"

She nods, sliding her hands up my chest to balance on me before leaning in and pressing our mouths together. My hand moves from her jaw to her nape as she parts her lips slightly, letting me deepen the kiss. She tastes like ice cream, bourbon, and possibility. But I pull away before I get myself into trouble I can't come back from.

"Andy is out for the night, dog sitting in Pac Heights," she says, fingering my tie, her breathing a little ragged.

Too late.

Chapter 9

Liv

I tug Owen through my door and am thrilled when he pushes me up against it.

"Liv," he breathes into my neck, his hands already skating down my body, over my curves. *Thank god.* I've never had to wonder if a guy was into me—until tonight. The way Owen's hand grazed my back protectively, the glint in his eye, the slow trace of his thumb over mine at the gala—it all felt real. But I've also never pretended to date someone before, and maybe Owen's just a fantastic actor.

I hadn't wanted our night to end, but I was ready to say goodnight at my door, thank him for his service, and never see him again...until he asked to kiss me like a goddamn cinnamon roll.

Now his mouth is consuming mine, soft and hungry. His hand drags up to cup my breast, and my nipples tighten under the thin fabric of my dress. He squeezes just hard enough to make me gasp out his name.

"Owen."

"Is this okay?" he asks as his mouth moves down the column of my throat. He shoves his jacket off my shoulders into a heap on the floor.

"Please," I tip my head back to give him access, and his teeth skim across my collarbone, sending a shudder across my skin.

Okay, not a cinnamon roll.

My hands tangle in his hair, and I pull his mouth back to mine, wanting to taste the bourbon on his tongue, wanting to feel more of his body pressed into mine, wanting more. I catch his lip with my teeth, and his groan slides down my throat.

Without breaking our kiss, he bunches my dress up my thighs, and he pushes his hips into me, locking me between the door and his erection.

"Yes," I gasp into his kiss, my hands working between us to untuck his shirt. He leans back just enough to let me, his fingers gripping the sides of my bare thighs.

"Tell me what you want," he murmurs, his green eyes—now a deep emerald—locking on mine. My gaze flicks down my body, just for a moment, before traveling back up to find his desire unmistakable.

"Goddamnit, Liv," he growls. "Hold this." He thrusts the rumpled fabric of my dress into my hands. I clutch the burgundy silk, lifting it a little higher, exposing my black lace underwear like a vintage can-can dancer.

"Goddamnit," he repeats under his breath and drops to his knees.

I stay frozen, holding my dress up, my heart hammering against my ribs. He sits back on his heels, hands on his thighs, his hooded eyes gazing up at me, pupils so blown they're nearly black.

"Lean back," he instructs, and I do. I rest my back against the door, but I can't take my eyes off his face. "You are mesmerizing," he says, awed.

"Owen…" My voice is hoarse. I'm not sure what I want to ask for, or maybe I am.

"Let me taste you." he says, low, steady, and full of heat. It doesn't sound like a question. It lands like a command, sending a shiver down my spine. And god, I want to obey. I nod. He leans forward and cups my hips, kissing the skin just below my belly button. "Use your words, Liv," he whispers into my skin. *Fuck.*

"I want to feel your mouth on me."

He kisses my pubic bone over the top of my underwear, about three inches higher than I want him. "Good girl," he praises, and my legs almost give out. His chuckle vibrates my skin as he moves his kisses to the top of my thighs and slides his hands around to the curve of my ass, kneading the flesh. He nips at the skin of my hip bones, and I want to thread my fingers in his hair and direct him where I want him, but I can't because I'm still holding my dress, and I somehow think that was by design. I also can't see what he's doing, but his mouth is warm against the crease of my hip before he presses a kiss between my thighs. I let out a moan.

Owen hooks his fingers into my underwear and slides them down my body, using his hand on my hip to help me step out of them. Before I put my second foot down, he guides my leg over his shoulder. I feel a little like a baby deer, perched on one heel-clad foot, but Owen's hand on my hip and my weight balanced on his shoulder stabilize me.

"Gorgeous," he murmurs from under my dress before his tongue presses flat against my slit, and my whole body pulls tight.

"Oh, god," I scream out as Owen sucks my clit into his mouth and I'm relieved that apartment 1A is vacant because there is no way the entire complex didn't just hear me.

"That's right, sweetheart," Owen coaxes, between flut-terings of his tongue and nips of his teeth. I let one hand drop my dress, and it cascades over his shoulder, but he doesn't break his rhythmic devouring of my clit, sucking and twirling and breaching my entrance.

"Owen, oh god," I say between breathy gasps, and he plunges two fingers inside with no warning, rough and perfect. And I come apart. My orgasm blindsides me, and my whole body convulses. He continues to lick and nip between my legs until I'm boneless.

I tug at his hair, desperate to have him up here, desperate to kiss him, and he complies, rising and taking my face in his hands. He kisses me hard, sucking my lip and licking into my mouth. I can taste myself, and it's fucking hot.

My hands find his belt, and I fumble to get it off, pulling it free in a long, whipping sound. Owen never stops kissing me, his mouth rough, his tongue searching. I can't help myself, and I palm him through his dress pants.

"Goddammit, Liv," he groans, and I love knowing his curse word of choice. I unzip his pants and slide my hand beneath the elastic band, finally gripping him. I squeeze, he slams his hand against the door over my head, and I jump a little. "Sorry," he murmurs, regaining his composure and returning to his more gentle demeanor, kissing me carefully, while I stroke his impressive length.

"I like it, Owen." I bite his lip a little to reinforce my statement. He groans, and I stroke him harder.

"You have to stop," he grits into my mouth, then slides his hands under my ass, like he plans to hoist me into his arms. "Can I take you to bed?"

"No," I say, cupping his face, pulling his mouth to mine. Owen stills, and my post-orgasm brain catches up to what I said. "I mean, I want to...right here." I kiss him again, and I can almost feel the moment my words click into place in his brain. He slams me back against the door, and I yank at my dress to give him access. His erection presses against my thigh, but he waits.

"Are you sure?" he murmurs, as I lick the skin below his jaw. "You don't owe me anything."

I pause for a moment, and so does Owen, searching my face, and I can only imagine what I look like. My lips are swollen, almost bruised, my hair is wild, and I'm sure my mascara is smudged, but I strangely don't mind.

"I feel...safe with you," I say, a little vulnerable, "like I can be a little messy and a little frantic and you won't mind."

"Not at all, Button," he says and kisses me gently this time. For several minutes, we're tender, languid. His fingers thread in my hair, my back pressed against the door to my apartment. I'm not wearing underwear, and his fly is undone, but other than that, we're both fully clothed.

"Owen," I say between kisses, "I want you inside me now."

He takes a moment to fish a condom from his wallet, and I push at his waistband until his pants pool on the floor. Then he hoists me into his arms, his forearm braced under my ass. I wrap my legs around his waist and kiss his neck. I can feel his dick against my slick entrance and every nerve ending in my body is already singing.

"Please," I am fully aware I'm begging now, but I need him closer.

Owen swears again under his breath and shifts my weight, spreading me so wide, my muscles burn. I have a bed, and there's a couch ten steps away. Hell, there's a counter next to us, but Owen follows my wishes, shifting me again until I feel him press into me. My body is open to him, I'm soaked, and my legs are splayed wide around his waist, but there is still a delightful strain as he enters me, a slow stretch. I arch my back against the door, a little whimper escaping my lips.

"You okay?"

"More." I try to pull him to me with my calf around his back.

"Unreal," he says, dropping his head to my breastbone once he's fully seated. "You feel so god dammed unreal."

I am full, exquisitely full, of Owen and of the gasps of air I'm trying to pull in when he begins to move his hips. This angle, this position, has him so deep inside me, he's hitting every possible nerve ending. My back banging into the door with every thrust, his fingers digging into the flesh of my ass where he's gripping me. I hope I can see his fingerprints tomorrow.

My fingers scrape at his shoulders, and he responds by thrusting rougher. Once, twice, three earnest thrusts before he drops my feet to the ground and spins me in one quick movement. Pushing me against the door with a hand flat against my spine, kissing the hollow behind my ear, and reaching around to cup my breast again.

"I just need..." I wiggle my ass back into his lap and he tucks my dress up over my hips, wedging himself back between my thighs. I'm so wet he slips in easily this time, and he grabs my hip bones, slamming me back against him. I'm not going to last. I can tell from his labored breath, he's close too. He reaches around my waist and presses hard and fast circles on my clit until I cry out and he shudders his release behind me.

He spins me around again and finds my mouth, holding my chin and devouring my kisses. I slump against the wall, and he peppers me with kisses on my cheekbone, my ear, my eyelids.

I want him to scoop me into his arms and carry me to bed. I want him to crawl in next to me and hold me until four a.m., when I want to wake up with his head between my thighs. Then I want him to stay until morning, kiss me awake, and make me believe this is more than it is. But it's not. This is pretend. And some very real, very good casual sex. That's all it can be.

Because I'm not the girl you stick it out for. I'm the one who needs a fake fiancé—because the real ones eventually leave. I'm too much work and somehow never enough. The one who lets you down or falls short of what you hoped I'd be.

"I should get cleaned up," I say, turning away from his kisses. Owen's lips trail after mine like a magnet until I gently touch his chest.

"Oh, right," he says, pulling back and zipping up his pants. "Right, I should...I should go."

"Yeah, probably," I say, smoothing my dress down.

Chapter 10

Owen

"Then you just left?"

"What was I supposed to do, Eli? Beg her to let me stay the night? Even I'm not that pathetic." I sit at Eli's small kitchen table, morning light filtering through the window. He pours hot water from the gooseneck kettle into the French press and grabs two mugs from the shelf. He says nothing, but I can tell he wants to. This is Eli—it's like pulling teeth to get anything out of him.

"Just say it," I say.

"Nothing." The timer on his phone dings, and he plunges the press of the coffee carafe down before filling two mugs. He pushes one across to me with a carton of oat milk and the sugar jar. He takes his black, like his soul.

"Fine. Do you have pages to show me?" I ask with more edge to my tone than I mean.

"How long have we known each other?" Eli asks, not answering my question.

"Eight excruciating years," I say, but Eli catches my smile.

"Eight years, so we know each other pretty well." Eli takes a long sip from his mug, then turns to the sink and fills a glass with water. He tips it into the plant on the shelf above the faucet, sets the glass in the dishwasher, and takes another drink of coffee.

"Eli." I wait for him to look at me. "Can you please finish your thought?"

I'm bracing for one of his classics—how I don't understand women, how I always misread the signs. Maybe he'll bring up that time I thought the barista was flirting with me, only for her to tap the tip jar. Or how my ex left me to go back to her boyfriend, saying I was too clingy. He wasn't being mean, just trying to remind me of the long list of ways I've managed to screw this up before.

But that's the thing—I didn't push Liv. I respected her boundaries. She was ready for the night to end, so I let it.

Was I disappointed? Yeah. I liked her. I thought we clicked. The sex was great, really great, but it was more than that. It was the way the conversation flowed, how easy it felt. She said I made her feel safe. And then she asked me to leave.

"Why don't you think I can write any pages?" Eli stares past me out the window. That's not where I thought he was going. He takes another sip of coffee, then rounds the counter and sinks into the chair across from me, like he's actually waiting for an answer.

"Um…" I'd armchair-quarterbacked Eli's writer's block a million times. Was it fear of failure? Was it stubbornness? Boredom? Was he afraid he'd peaked after winning a Pulitzer at twenty-five? It was probably all of those and none of those, and he already knew that. But I say, "I think sometimes it's hard to live up to the expectations we have of ourselves in our minds."

Eli nods. "I think maybe you could have asked to see her again."

"Did you just reverse psychology me?"

Eli laughs. "You know how you tell me it's okay to write shitty pages? That my next book doesn't need to win a Pulitzer?"

"What's your analogy here? Who's the shitty pages in this story?"

"I'm no expert. God knows I haven't been on a date in years, probably longer than you—"

"I did have sex just last night, mind you."

"Yeah, yeah, don't rub it in."

"I'm pretty sure the way dating works is you meet someone you find interesting, and you hang out. Then you ask to see them again." Eli gets up from the table and tops off his coffee. "You two started unconventionally. Maybe she felt weird after having sex with her fake date. You could just send her a text saying you'd like to see her again...for real this time."

"I don't know, Eli. She didn't seem interested in anything more last night."

"Did she tell you to leave?"

I replay the night in my mind, how I was completely enamored with her brilliance, how she looked in my jacket, how soft her skin felt under my hands, and the little mews of pleasure she made during her orgasms. And how she told me she needed to get cleaned up...and I told her I should leave.

"Fuck," I mutter, not meeting Eli's eyes.

"Call the manager at Benu and say you are Elijah Thorne's agent and you want a table for two tonight. There's usually a three-month wait."

I sigh and put my head in my hands.

"Or take her on a private helicopter ride around the bay at sunset. That will impress her."

But I don't think it will. I think about the gala last night, the fake faces, and the even faker attitudes. That isn't Liv; she's genuine, down-to-earth, and...real.

"When was the last time you left this house?" I ask Eli, raising my head.

"I went to the gym at six a.m. yesterday," Eli says defiantly.

"Under the cloak of darkness," I laugh. "Okay, I'll make you a deal. If you leave the apartment without headphones, and say ten words to literally anyone else besides me and the guy who delivers your acai bowls, I'll text Liv and at least give her the option of seeing me again."

"The guy who delivers my acai bowls leaves them on my doorstep," Eli says, draining the last of his coffee.

I huff out a laugh. "Alright, let's sweeten the deal. If you chicken out, I get to drive Sally on my date tonight."

"Now you're full of confidence on a second date."

I shrug, "I'm calling it our first."

"You've already slept with her."

"So we have a deal?" I ask, holding out my hand and ignoring his comment.

Eli shakes my hand, but his eyes flick toward his office in the apartment's second bedroom. Like suddenly, he has work to do.

Chapter 11

Liv

"Then he just left?"

Andy hops up on my desk and swings her feet, picking up a Zelda action figurine I keep on my desk for good luck.

"Andy, it was a fake date."

"That ended in a mind-blowing orgasm."

I try to keep my eyes on my computer, but I know my smirk gives me away.

"Multiple orgasms?!?" She glances across our living room. "I'll never be able to look at our front door again without thinking about you getting railed against it."

"Yeah, sorry about that." I try to resume typing.

"No, thank you, Lemon Pie, you're my sex hero. While I was spooning a labradoodle, you were crashing the custard truck in our kitchen."

I nearly spit out my oat milk latte, choking on a laugh. "I—" I gasp, wiping my mouth, "I don't even know what that means—" Another burst of laughter escapes. "But please, *please* don't ever say it again."

"What? You got your butter churned. Good for you." Andy shrugs and jumps off my desk. "When do you plan to board the boney express again?"

I can not catch my breath, but shake my head, "I don't think I'll be boarding..." I wave my hand, "I don't think I'll be seeing him again at all."

"I thought you had a good time?" she asks, pulling open the refrigerator door and emerging with a handful of grapes and a Diet Coke.

"I did." The memory of the night rushes in—how he actually listened when I talked about my work, how easily he opened up about his family. And I can still feel his hands on my body, the way he seemed to know exactly what I needed at every moment of the night. "But he seemed pretty ready to leave after we were, um...finished."

"So, is he upstairs with the recluse right now?" Andy asks, heading for the door.

"Adeline Vale, so help me god."

"What? I want to see inside that guy's apartment...do you think there's like a sex dungeon?"

"A dungeon on the third floor? You know, those two are the nicest apartments in the building."

"Yeah, and your man is up there."

"He's not my man. It was a one-night thing."

"So let's count this off," Andy says, ticking her fingers. "He agrees to fake date you, does actual homework, and now knows more about you than I do. Then he stands up to the Wicked Witch of Nob Hill, takes you out for arguably the best pizza in the City, and then makes you come in our entry-way—twice—and *you* don't want to see him again?"

"It's not that I don't," I say. "It's that 'again' wasn't part of the agreement."

"There it is."

"What?"

"Fake dating is a pretty convenient excuse for you."

"What does that mean?"

"It means fake also means safe. If it was just sex, that's fine—you don't owe him or anyone more than that," Andy says, then her voice softens, "but, Lemon Drop...you've been taught to think love has to be earned. What if Owen's the first one who makes you feel like you're already enough?"

"I've known him for, like, thirty-seven minutes."

"So call him. Get to know him for thirty-eight. Scare the hell out of yourself—because I think deep down, you want something real."

I roll my eyes, mostly to stall. Because damn it, she's not wrong. My chest tightens with something like hope, but what if I'm reading him wrong? What if I get it wrong again?

"I don't know." I take a sip of my latte to have something to do besides confront my feelings.

"I'm just saying the object of your clunge plunge is pretty much thirty feet above your head."

This time, coffee actually dribbles out of my mouth. I walk over to the sink to get a napkin when my phone pings back on my desk.

"Oh my god," Andy says, reading my text and holding the phone out to me.

Owen: *Liv, I really enjoyed being your fake date last night. I'm sorry I left abruptly. I wonder if I could take you on a real date tonight? If not, no hard feelings. But if so, I'll pick you up at 7 —O*

Andy stares at me with a knowing smirk. "Guess I'm spooning a labradoodle again."

Owen is holding a tiny succulent when I open my door to his knock at exactly 7 p.m.

"You said you couldn't keep a plant alive, but I think the others didn't try hard enough. This one's a fighter," he says, holding it out. He's wearing jeans and his signature hint of a blush.

"Thanks." I take the little plant, and he catches my wrist and pulls me in for a quick kiss on the cheek.

"It's good to see you again," he says. "Thank you for agreeing to this."

I'm distracted by the kiss and by the way his forearms flex where the sleeves of his black button-down are rolled back to his elbows. It's the most casual I've seen him, and somehow he still looks effortlessly put together.

"I'm not sure what I've agreed to," I try to laugh, but my heart is hammering in my chest. Last night, we attempted to trick an entire gala of my parents' closest friends into believing that we were engaged, but I'm somehow more nervous about tonight. "Am I dressed okay?" I ask, looking down at my jeans and v-neck sweater, the one Andy says makes my boobs look like globes of cantaloupe.

"You look beautiful," he says as his eyes quickly scan my body in a way that makes my insides tighten. "I figured we did fancy for our fake date. I wanted this one to be a little more..." he pauses, and I can't help but finish his sentence in my head with 'real,' but he finishes, "low-key."

"I don't remember a convertible yesterday?" I ask when we reach the curb of my building, eying the vintage Mustang with the top down.

"No," he laughs, "I had a rental Corolla yesterday. But I wanted something a little more fun for tonight. Besides, Eli never drives it."

"This is Elijah Thorne's vintage Mustang?" I say. "And he's letting you drive it?"

"He lost a bet," he says with a smirk and holds the door open for me. Once he's in the driver's seat, he hands me a pair of cheap gas station-style sunglasses. They are oversized and...bright yellow. "I thought these would look perfect on you," he says, and the way he smiles at me makes something flutter low in my chest. "And there are hair rubber bands in the cup holder, if you need one. It gets a little windy on the Great Highway."

I pull my loose waves into a quick braid and glance over, only to see Owen wearing a matching pair of sunglasses, completely straight-faced. I lose it, double over with laughter, and an actual snort escapes before I can stop it.

"What?" he says, easing away from the curb. "I thought they looked good with my complexion."

We park in a nondescript neighborhood in the Avenues, a few blocks up from the beach. Owen puts up the top and guides me with his hand at the base of my spine into a little shack-like structure with a faded sign reading "Mama's" over the door. It smells like grease, sea salt, and deliciousness.

At the counter, Owen orders two orders of fish and chips, looking at me for confirmation. I nod.

"I don't know what you've heard," he says with a little wink, "but I believe crispy food equals joy."

He carries our plastic baskets lined with paper, already soaking up grease from the massive pile of fries and huge pieces of battered fish. It smells like heaven. I bring our two frozen lemonades, and we find a picnic table on the back deck. It's chilly; the fog has rolled in. But Mama's has Mexican-style woven blankets and overhead gas heaters at each table.

"Oh my god," I say around a huge mouthful of fried fish.

"I know, right?" Owen says, popping more fries into his mouth than will politely fit, and I love it.

Conversation flows like we've done this a hundred times. Owen tells me about growing up in small-town Ohio—about snow days and basement bands. I fill him in on the least glamorous details of RootDown's latest launch. But he listens like I'm recounting a moon landing, nodding at all the right places, eyes lit with interest.

We trade jokes between bites, and at some point, I swipe a fry from his basket despite having more than enough of my own. He slides the whole thing my way, barely pausing the story of how he and Eli met and how he basically lied his way into a job as his agent when they were both twenty-two.

He's a natural storyteller, but what gets me is how tuned in he is. He asks real questions—the kind that make me feel seen, not scanned. I tell him about the time Spenser tried to teach me to surf at Ocean Beach when I was fifteen, how we bailed after one wave, got donuts, and skipped school. He forged our dad's signature so I wouldn't get caught. We never told anyone.

Owen laughs—not just at the story, but like he remembers it too, like he's been here all along.

"Ready for stop two?" Owen asks, tossing our dinner remnants in the trash and stacking the baskets on top. I nod, slurping the last sip of my lemonade.

We walk a few blocks until Owen stops in front of what appears to be an abandoned storefront, the windows blacked out. Above the door is a small hand-lettered sign that reads, "The Library." But something about the glint in Owen's eyes makes me think we won't find books inside. He holds the door open for me, and I can't believe what I see—or hear—when we walk in.

Every possible vintage arcade game flashes its neon lights and chimes its musical tunes. *Donkey Kong*, *Ms. Pac-Man*, and *Mortal Kombat*—all the games I had to sneak over to the neighbor's to play as a kid.

"What is this place?" I say in awe.

Owen holds out his fist and drops a handful of coins into my palm. "Let's see what you got, Arden."

I beat him at *everything*: *Pole Position*, *Street Fighter*, and even *Whack-a-Mole*. I can tell by the concentration in his brows and the curse words he lets slip that he's not letting me win. He feigns sulking, claiming the games are rigged and demanding a rematch. We play another round, and he finally beats my score—once—at *Pac-Man*. He dances around the arcade, pumping his fists in the air. He uses his meager ticket winnings to buy me a tiny Princess Peach statue when I explain she was the actual hero of the Mario Brothers game.

"Everyone thinks she's just sitting there waiting to be rescued," I tell him, eyeing my new three-inch-tall best friend. "But she's surviving, keeping the kingdom together, and when she gets the chance, she saves the day herself. That's the real hero to me."

My heart swells at the thoughtfulness of this entire date; he's known me for less than forty-eight hours, and he's more tuned into me than anyone in my family has ever been. I have a few coins left in my pocket, so I tug him into the photo booth. He pulls me onto his lap as I feed the coins into the slot, wrapping his hands around my waist. We take a normal photo, then silently agree to make silly faces for the next two. Before the last flash goes off, I turn to look at him. His smile is so disarming that I forget to breathe for a moment, then I grab his face and kiss him just as the last flash goes off. He kisses me back, but it's slow and unhurried, his hand trailing feather-light across the bare skin at my waist where my sweater has hitched. He tastes like salt and the Junior Mints we shared from the vending machine.

He gently pulls away, and I try to lean in, but he tips his chin down to the two pairs of shoes waiting outside the photo booth curtain. "On to stop three?" he asks, his voice soft.

We stop at the Mustang, and Owen first hands me an oversized hoodie from the backseat before popping the trunk to reveal a blanket, a small bundle of firewood, and a bag of marshmallows. He takes our supplies out and squints up at the darkening horizon.

"I think my competitive streak might have made us miss the sunset."

"That's okay," I say, taking the blanket from him. "This part's my favorite—when everything gets quiet and golden."

Twenty minutes later, he has a small but mighty fire going, and we are skewering fat marshmallows, sitting close together on the blanket against the chilly night. My first one immediately catches fire and plops into the coals. Owen chuckles and skewers a new one for me. I stick it back in the fire, concentrating on rotating it to keep it from burning again.

"I can admit you totally schooled me at the arcade," Owen says, blowing on his perfectly roasted marshmallow. "But you're about to burn your second one, so let me help." He slides the gooey blob off his stick and holds it out. I part my lips, letting him feed it to me, and I swear I hear his breath catch. He's about to pull his hand away when I grab his wrist.

"I missed some," I say, pulling his finger back to my mouth to suck the sticky sugar off.

"Liv..." His hand snakes around the nape of my neck, and he pulls me close. He presses a kiss to my mouth, and his lips are soft, yet the kiss is demanding. And I don't mind. "I want my own taste," he says, licking into my mouth. "So sweet." He kisses me again before moving down my jaw and sucking the skin at the juncture of my neck. "And here, tastes so good."

I want to be closer, so I clamber over and straddle his lap. He continues to kiss every piece of exposed skin he can find.

"So I guess we've kind of done this backwards, huh?" I breathe out, tipping my head back when he drags his teeth across my throat.

"First, you were my husband, then we got engaged, then you met my mother—sorry about that, by the way—then we slept together...and now we're on our first date?"

"Making out like teenagers on the beach," he laughs, lowering me back onto the blanket. "So, what comes next?"

"Maybe you'll be the one to hit on me in a bar," I say, my voice a little lower.

"Maybe I already did," he says into my mouth, before moving his kisses down the column of my throat to the ridge of my clavicle. "I was drawn to you. I saw you across the bar before that asshole even came over." His hands are now exploring under my shirt, squeezing my breasts. He pushes the fabric of my bra aside to find my nipples already peaked with arousal.

"Why didn't you invite me up to your room?" I pant out while he continues to kiss the swell of my breast and roll my nipple between his thumb and finger.

"I have no fucking idea."

"You could take me there now."

Chapter 12

Owen

"I'm all sandy and I smell like grease," she says as I slide the key card into my hotel room door. "Would you mind if I took a quick rinse-off shower?"

"I think you smell delicious," I tell her, kissing the hollow behind her ear. "But of course. You get in the shower, and I'll call for more towels."

We walk to the hotel room, and it's almost bizarre how comfortable we both seem. Liv kicks off her sandals in front of the closet and reaches her hand behind her neck to stretch. I can't take my eyes off the soft curve of her neck. I want to lean in and press a quiet kiss there.

She offers me a gentle smile, and it's like we're coming back to *our* hotel room after a day of being tourists on a couple's getaway. She's going to take a shower while I order room service, and then we'll get into bed to eat French fries and cuddle. I'll rub her feet, sore from walking around and seeing the sights all day, and the foot rub will turn into more intimate caresses, evolving into lazy vacation lovemaking. Suddenly, that's all I want.

"What?" She looks at me laughing, and I realize I've been staring at her during my daydream.

"Nothing." I look down, and I know I'm blushing.

"You are pretty adorable," she says, coming close and wrapping her arms around my neck.

"I'm not sure if adorable is a compliment a man likes to hear," I chuckle, but I grip her waist and kiss her slowly.

"It is." She pulls back and smiles, and all I can think is—I want to remember this. The crinkle in her eyes, that perfect bow of her lip. I want to carry it with me, always. "I'll be right back." She gives me another quick kiss and disappears into the bathroom.

The water turns on, and of course, I'm picturing her naked on the other side of the door. But I'm also picturing waking up next to her tomorrow, all sleep-mussed and warm skin pressed against mine. And I'm almost as excited about that.

Last night was fast and frantic and hot as fuck, but I want to take my time tonight. I want to revisit all the ways I've learned to make her gasp and sigh, and I want to spend hours—maybe the rest of my life—learning all the other ways to please her.

When housekeeping delivers the towels, I momentarily wonder what to do with them. I knock gently on the bathroom door. "I'll leave your towels on the hook here."

"You can come in," she calls through the closed door. My pulse rate increases, and I'm instantly hard. *Chill the fuck out, dude.* I step into the steamy little room and set the towels on the sink. "Here you go," I say, and start to back out.

"Stay," she says. "I want to talk."

"Okay," I say, a little unsure, and lean against the counter. "Everything okay?"

"Yeah," she pokes her head out from behind the shower curtain. She's all wet and flushed, and soap bubbles are dripping down the side of her face. "I just want to talk more." Then she tucks herself back into her shower. "How did you decide to become a literary agent?"

"Oh, I—" My insides heave with how much I love this. "I wanted to be a writer in college. I attended a panel discussion about the publishing industry, but I was more fascinated by the agent on the panel. I went up to her after the talk, and while everyone else was asking if they could pitch their book idea, I asked if she would tell me how I could do her job."

"Really?" she asks from inside the cloud of steam. "That's so cool. What did she say?"

"She offered to meet for coffee, and then offered me an internship when I finished school, and then offered me a job. I'm still with her agency today. It's worked out pretty well."

"That is wild to me," Liv says. The water shuts off, and suddenly I panic, heading for the door. She pulls back the shower curtain, still blocking most of her body, but I can see the curve of her bare hip and the swell of her breast behind the thin curtain, and my breath catches. "Hand me a towel," she holds out her hand, and I do.

"I've had, like, a million different jobs," she says, stepping out of the shower and tucking the towel between her breasts. Her skin is pink and flushed and still damp, and I want to lick off every water droplet from her body. "And you've had one job since college?"

"I guess I've always known what I wanted when it was right in front of me."

Liv looks up from where she's rubbing a towel through her hair, and her gaze catches on mine. She pulls her lip between her teeth, like she did that first night at the bar. This time, though, I reach out and glide my thumb across it, coaxing it free, and let my thumb linger against the soft curve of her mouth.

"What do you want right now?" she says, her voice a little breathy.

I push off the counter and scoop her body into my arms. She lets out a delighted squeal.

"You in my bed," I say, and walk out of the bathroom.

She had pinned her hair up to keep it dry in the shower, so when I lay her down on the bed, her brown waves fan out on my pillow, just like my fantasy. Only the real thing is a million times better.

She gestures for me to join her on the bed and I climb on next to her.

"Last night was hot," she says, lacing her hand with mine and tugging me down, "but I want to take our time tonight."

"Button, we have all the time in the world."

We don't kiss right away. Instead, we both look at each other like we're looking beyond our faces, right into each other's souls. My hand grazes the delicate line of her jaw, and she leans into it like she's been waiting her whole life to be touched exactly like this. I drag my thumb across her cheekbone and her eyes flutter closed.

"I like the way you touch me."

"I like touching you." I trace my finger across her collarbone before bending down and pressing my mouth to that spot on her neck I've been eyeing all night. She lets her head roll to the side, giving me access, and I kiss up the column of her throat, to the soft spot behind her ear.

"I want you to touch me more," she says and places my hand flat against her chest, right above the knot of her towel. Her heartbeat flutters under my fingers, a little fast and erratic, and I could die right now knowing I have this effect on her body. I untuck the towel from between her breasts, but leave it draped over her body. She's like a present, and I want to take my time unwrapping her.

Her hands fist around the hem of my shirt, tugging me closer, and I let her peel it off me before pressing my mouth to hers. She tastes like marshmallows and bourbon and everything else I've ever craved.

"Whatever you want, Liv. Let me give it to you."

I kiss down her body to where her towel is draped over her chest. She takes the edges and opens it, revealing her gorgeous honey skin, still flushed from the shower. I'm captivated by the rise of her perfect curves, her pebbled nipples, the most delicious shade of peach, waiting for my mouth. Last night, we never got our clothes off. Now she's splayed before me, completely naked, like an offering to the gods, and I will bow at their altar every day for this woman.

"Fuck, Liv, look at you," I say with mind-numbing reverence. I lower my mouth to her breast and suck her nipple into my mouth. She sighs my name, and I feel it inside my chest.

I knead and massage one breast while my tongue flicks across the other peaked nipple. Her nails drag through my hair with a delightful scrape, and I use my teeth to apply a little pressure, testing her boundaries.

"Yes," she breathes out and pulls my mouth tighter to her. I bite down just enough to make her gasp, then soothe the spot with my tongue.

Her breath hitches as my hand travels down the curve of her waist until it finds its home between her thighs. I had wanted to take my time, but the way she arches into my touch, trusting and needy, I can't make her wait. Hell, I can't wait. I slip my finger into her core, and she is so wet and ready for me, I immediately add a second finger.

She gasps my name, and I nearly lose it at the rawness in her voice.

My mouth finds hers again, deeper this time. Not rushed. Just...greedy. Like I've waited years for this.

My fingers pump with a slow, deliberate rhythm. And she whimpers these little mewls of pleasure. My dick is so hard, caged against the fly of my jeans that it is almost painful, but I can tell she's close and there is no way I'm going to stop.

"Owen," she gasps, "harder."

I take her breast back into my mouth and suck and flick and nip until she's writhing underneath me. Circling her clit faster with my thumb and pushing down with the pressure I now know she craves.

Her muscles begin to clench around me and I pull back enough to look at her, because damn if I'm going to miss the way she looks when she crashes at my touch.

Her body trembles with these little aftershocks of her pleasure, and I pull her into my arms and stroke her cheek and the skin of her ribs. That I made her come apart feels like a privilege, not a right—and I plan to earn it, every time.

She rolls into me and buries her face in my chest, and I'm pretty sure she inhales. I hope I smell like her. She fumbles with the button of my pants, and I chuckle at her post-orgasm lack of dexterity.

"Do you need some help, Button?" I kiss her temple.

"Can you take these off, please?" she says, a little exasperated.

"You tell me what you need, Liv," I say, rolling onto my back and undoing my zipper. "Say the word and it's yours. Every time."

She helps me slip out of my pants and underwear, and my dick springs to attention. I'm momentarily embarrassed by how hard I am for her, but she just smiles.

"Looks like we have the same effect on each other," she says before she palms me in a few hard strokes. I groan, grab a condom off the nightstand, and pull her on top of me.

She sits up, her thighs bracketing my hips, and she looks like a goddess. Her cheeks are flushed, her hair is wild, and she's slick against me. She moves, grinding against me, and her eyes close again, her head tipping back.

"Yes, there you go, sweetheart. Take what you need."

"I need you inside me," she says, and she rises on her knees and positions me at her entrance. Then she locks eyes with me and slowly, so fucking slowly, lowers herself down on me until I'm so impossibly deep. Both of us are wound so tight that neither of us moves, or else we'll both explode.

When our breathing has slowed, she begins to rock, controlling the pace and the angle and her own pleasure while

I get to watch and feel her slick and tight around me. I place my hands on her thighs and squeeze, silently encouraging her to keep going. Then my hands slide around the curve of her ass to pull her tighter against me.

It feels so damn good.

We both are spiraling up, and I'm ready to follow her over the edge, when she slows her pace again and catches her breath. I can't help but marvel at all that she is above me and around me.

"The way you're looking at me right now—" she says, opening her eyes, locking her gaze with mine.

"Is it too much?"

"No," she leans forward and kisses me, "I don't think I've ever felt more seen in my life."

She rests her head against my forehead, her fingers curling around the back of my neck like she's anchoring to me, like she wants me to stay. Forever.

Usually, I fall fast and burn out faster. But this...this is steadier. Like settling into something real. She doesn't need saving. She doesn't need me to fix a damn thing. She just wants me. And I want her. Maybe—for once—that's enough.

"Owen, can you—"

"Yeah, I got you." I move beneath her, taking over the work, but she's still in control. God, she's in control. She sits back up, and I reach between our bodies, and she grinds against my knuckles, her breasts bouncing with each thrust.

"Everything about you is perfect," I say, picking up my pace when I can tell she's getting close.

"I don't want to be perfect," she breathes out just before coming. "I want to be real."

She unravels and folds over my body, letting out little cries as I drive up into her hard, chasing my own release. We're almost perfectly timed, like we were made for this. Like we were made for each other.

I pull her tight to my chest, kissing her temple and the line of her shoulder. She's still wrapped around my body, and I'm still inside her, and I don't plan on leaving anytime soon.

I want to tell her she is perfect, just as she is. I want to rage at her mother, her asshole ex, or anyone else in her life who made her feel like she wasn't enough or too much, or anything other than exactly who she is. But she doesn't want perfect.

"You don't have to pretend with me."

"You make me feel like I'm enough," she whispers into my neck. "I didn't realize how much I needed that...until you."

Chapter 13

Liv

I wake surrounded by a cozy nest of crisp sheets and Owen's arms. It was, hands down, the best sleep of my life, even if there wasn't much of it. We dozed after that first incredible round and then woke in the dark stillness of the night. Owen's hands mapped every curve of my naked body, then he retraced his path with his mouth until I unraveled while he watched from the v between my legs.

Now, I want to curl back into his side and drift off again, or, if I'm being honest, I want to crawl down his body and wake him up with my mouth. I checked the bedside clock. *Shit.* They are expecting me in the RootDown offices soon. I should have gotten more work done yesterday. I can't skimp today with the launch so close.

Owen stirs and bands his arms around me, tucking me into his big spoon, his erection presses against my bare ass as his sleepy hand comes up to squeeze my breast and he peppers my neck with kisses.

"I have to go," I whisper, but I also arch back into him.

"Then don't do that." His teeth graze my shoulder blade. "Or I'm going to need at least another hour between your thighs."

His hand trails down between my legs, and it does dangerous things to my ability to think straight. "I can't." I reluctantly push away from him and sit up.

"Okay," he rolls onto his back and smiles at me like I'm already the best part of his day. "I think you accidentally wore my sweatshirt home."

I look down at my naked breasts. A tiny mouth-shaped bruise blooms like a souvenir from the way he roughly but reverently handled me last night.

"I don't think I'm wearing a sweatshirt right now."

"Then wear it home and give it back to me when I see you tonight," he says, propping himself on an elbow while I shimmy back into my jeans.

"I'm seeing you tonight?" I raise my eyebrow at him, but I already know I am.

"Please, it's my last night in town. I have to go to DC early tomorrow."

We haven't talked about what that means, but I don't want to think about him leaving yet.

His sweatshirt smells like bourbon and campfire and contentment as I pull it over my head. The moment I lean down to kiss him, his arms circle my waist, rolling me back onto the tangle of sheets with him. He kisses me slow and deliberate, his hands splayed across my ribcage under his sweatshirt. His phone bursts into "We Are Family," and I pull back, laughing.

"I hate my sisters right now," he groans, throwing his arms over his face, while I climb off the bed and slip into my shoes.

"You talk to them now. I have to go." I bend down and kiss him quickly. "Pick me up at six."

He grabs my hand and places a kiss on the inside of my wrist. "I can't wait."

I slip out of the hotel room and hear a chorus of "Uncle Owen!" as I shut the door.

It's still early when I exit onto the street. The weather is perfect. It feels like the sun came out just for me.

I'd spent years convincing myself I didn't want anything real. Real always seemed like something I had to earn. But being with Owen feels easy. Like I don't have to try so hard or be "on" all the time. Maybe that's what *real* actually is. Maybe I'm finally ready to believe that someone could want me exactly as I am, no fixing required.

Santa Barbara is only a five-hour drive and barely an hour flight. We both work from home. After this launch, I'll have more time. And his biggest client lives in my building, so surely we can make something work.

I'm halfway down the street when I pat my pocket, checking for the Princess Peach figurine Owen won me with his hard-earned arcade tickets last night. Standing in her power pose, she's destined for a prime spot on my desk, right next to Zelda—a tiny reminder to survive this launch, see Owen again tonight, and maybe even admit I want to keep seeing him...whatever that might mean.

But my pocket's empty. I pat my hips, check the back pockets—nothing. She must've slipped out when my pants hit the floor in last night's whirlwind. Owen's checking out in a few hours, and it's not like he'd think to look for her. That stupid little princess already means more to me than I want to admit. I could text him...but it'll be faster to run back upstairs and look for myself.

Owen's hotel room door is ajar as I approach. I must not have shut it all the way when I left.

"It's not like that, Kelc," Owen says, still on FaceTime as I pause outside his door.

"Owen, come on." His sister's voice carries through the speaker. "You always do this—you find a girl who needs saving, and suddenly you're all in. It's your thing. You're like a golden retriever puppy with a savior complex."

"This isn't like that. Liv's not—"

"Not like Melanie, who cried on your couch for three weeks until she went back to her boyfriend? Or Isla, who was madly in love with you but was really using you for connections?"

Owen sighs. "Yeah, but this feels different."

"You're a *good guy*, Owen. I know you *think* this is different. But you like a project. Hell, look at Eli! You think you can fix people, you take a risk, and they let you down." It's quiet for a long moment before she speaks again. "This one needed a fake date, and you stepped up...is this another girl who needs a little too much and makes you feel important?"

No. Owen told me I didn't have to pretend. He said he wanted me exactly as I am. And he's right—this feels different for me, too.

I can't hear what he's saying to his sister anymore, so I take a step closer, nudging the door open a little wider. He's taken her off speaker now. He's pulled on a pair of sweats and is standing near the window, his back to me, phone pressed to his ear. His head dips as he pinches the bridge of his nose.

"You're not wrong about my past," he says, almost too quiet for me to catch. "And maybe it was just a fake date."

My fingers curl into a fist as I take a step back. Of course. That's what this is. I'm the mess. The project. The girl who needs too much. And he's just another guy who thinks loving me is some kind of rescue mission.

I don't need to hear another word. I turn and walk away.

Chapter 14

Owen

"It might have started that way, Kelcy," I say, taking a steadying breath to keep my voice even. I rarely push back on either of my sisters, but this matters too much to stay quiet. "But my feelings aren't fake." I go on, a little steadier. "I know you're trying to protect me. But Liv is the most competent, badass woman I've ever met. She doesn't need saving. She doesn't need me. She just...wants me. And I want her—not because she's a project, but because she's her."

"I don't want to see you get hurt," Kelcy says softly.

"Yeah, but...I might. That's life. But I'd rather risk something real than stay safe and miss it. Love isn't something you can control—I know, because I've tried. That's how I know this is different. I don't want to control it. I just don't want to miss it. I want all of her—exactly as she is."

Kelcy gives a quiet laugh. "Wow. I've never heard you say it like that."

I smile faintly, letting out a breath. "I appreciate you looking out for me. I always will. But you've got to trust me on this one, okay? You need to back off and let me figure out my own life."

"Fair enough," she says, her voice warm with reluctant approval.

"Your baby brother's growing up."

"Okay," my sister shifts the phone in her hand, "what's next?"

"I don't know. I'm going to see her tonight before I leave for DC early tomorrow morning to meet with Senator Langford, but maybe I can fly straight back to San Francisco this weekend."

"Okay, but...give her a little space. You've convinced me this might be different, but you can still be a lot sometimes."

"I'm hanging up now," I say with an eye roll. "Kiss my nephews."

An hour later, I'm heading to Eli's apartment when I pause at Liv's door. I consider knocking or leaving a note to let her know I'm thinking of her. But my sister's right. Liv's in the middle of a huge launch, and I've already distracted her enough this weekend, plus I only have one day left with Eli before I have to leave. I can go eight hours without seeing her.

"Hey!" the guy from the other day calls out as I hit the second-floor landing. He's stepping out of his apartment with another man, taller than both of us. "You're friends with Liv, right? And Eli?" He offers a handshake. "I'm Cal." He reminds me and gestures to the guy beside him. "This is my buddy, Liam." Then back to me. "Owen, right?"

"Yeah, that's right," I say, shaking Cal's hand and turning to his friend. "Nice to meet you."

Cal is tall, but Liam is huge. His shoulders are almost wider than the doorway.

"You too, man," Liam says, returning my handshake. "Do you live in the building?"

"No," I say, but an image flashes—waking up next to Liv every morning, making her coffee, curling up to watch a movie at night. Sharing little wins, venting about our rough days. I shake my head, trying to push away the echo of my sister's voice: *You move too fast.* "Just visiting friends," I add.

"Liam is going to be staying in my apartment for the next couple of weeks," Cal explains, pushing the button on the keypad.

"Then I'm sure I'll see you in the building," I say. "I visit a lot." *And hopefully more*, I think.

Chapter 15

Liv

"Are we toasting launch success or drowning boy sorrows?" Andy asks, holding up her very fruity cocktail. I had texted her to meet me at Bar None at six sharp. I didn't want to be home.

"Both...neither," I say, shooting my bourbon like a shot of cheap tequila and placing it back on the bar, signaling for Frankie to fill it up.

"Okaaayy." Andy takes a sip of her pink drink. She plucks the orange wedge from the rim and sucks it between her teeth, watching me from the corner of her eye—but she doesn't push. She's good like that.

"Oh! I met the recluse yesterday," she says, popping one of the maraschino cherries into her mouth. "Strangely hot for a weirdo."

"I think his name is Eli," I say, sipping my second glass of bourbon with a little more decorum. I'm not sure if Eli wants people to know his alter ego, so I keep it at that.

"Yeah," she says, nodding. "He walked down the stairs right as I opened our door. I said 'hi,' and he came over, held out his hand, and said, 'I'm Eli. It's a nice day out.' Then he turned around, muttered—I swear Liv—'Fuck, that wasn't ten words,' and walked straight out of the building like he was trying to get away from me."

I huff out a pathetic laugh. "Owen said he's a little socially awkward." Saying Owen's name makes my heart pinch. I take another long sip of my drink.

"Yeah, I think I scared him," Andy says, shrugging her shoulders. "He had that whole tortured genius look going on. I was low-key into it. I might end up on his doorstep one of these days, like a lost puppy."

I stare into my drink. I can't respond to her antics at the moment.

She taps her nails against her glass, eyeing me with a mix of amusement and concern. "Sooo," she says slowly, "how was your date last night...and should I mention you're wearing last night's jeans?" She tries to sound casual, but I see it in her eyes—she's clocked the bourbon, the mood, and she's doing the math.

"I don't want to talk about it," I say, tipping my glass to my mouth again.

Andy puts her hand over the rim and nudges it back to the table.

"I know RootDown is about to IPO, but I don't think tomorrow you will be happy you're shooting thirty-dollar bourbon like it's Cuervo Silver."

My phone buzzes on the bar.

Owen: *Hey Liv, I'm at your apartment, but I don't think anyone's home. I'm sure you got busy with launch stuff. Let me know when you're free. I could grab us takeout.*

"Is this why we are hiding at Bar None on a Monday night?" Andy says, reading Owen's text.

"Maybe."

"I thought you agreed to try something real with him."

"Apparently, I was the *only* one who agreed to that. Some of us were still faking it."

I pick up my phone and type out a text.

Liv: Something came up. I think it's best if we call this what it was and go our separate ways. Thanks for fake-dating me, you were very convincing.

"What happened?" Andy grimaces, reading my text.

I watch the text bubbles appear and disappear until the screen goes blank. No reply.

"I don't know. I thought we were on the same page, but apparently, I was just some charity project. He has some kind of savior kink, and he was just swooping in to protect me from my 'mean mother.' Taking me to play stupid video games because I had a traumatic childhood."

Andy watches me rant over the rim of her glass, slurping her drink.

"How," she says carefully, "do you know this?"

"He said it, Andy. I heard him talking to his sister. She said he always does this, and I was just another girl who needs too much." I shoot the bourbon. Hell with it. "Sound fucking familiar?"

"Oh, Lambchop," Andy puts a comforting hand on my shoulder. "You know this is him, not you, right?"

"He's not the first guy to say I'm not low maintenance."

She picks up my phone and reads his text again. "Are you sure that's what he said?"

"Pretty much. Then he agreed it was all fake."

Andy looks like she's about to say something more, but something catches her eye over my shoulder.

"Oh, there's Cal and that hottie I've seen him with the past few days," Andy says, waving to our upstairs neighbor entering the bar.

"Hey, ladies," Cal says, coming up next to us. I don't feel like small talk, but Cal has always been a friendly neighbor. Kind of a big brother type.

"I'm Andy," she says, holding her hand out to Cal's friend. "It's a pleasure to meet me."

Cal and I both laugh quietly, and Cal says, "This is Liam. We've been best friends since ninth grade. He's going to be staying in my apartment while I'm gone on my next assignment."

"Well, we are downstairs if you need a cup of sugar." Andy bats her eyelashes, "Or a little spice. I'm versatile."

"Please excuse my roommate. I'm Liv," I say, shaking Liam's hand. "We try to keep her on a leash."

Andy shrugs. "I mean, I'm into it."

Cal waves Frankie over and orders two beers, "And whatever the ladies are drinking," he adds.

"Is this a girls' night, or want to grab a table?" Cal asks once we all have our drinks.

"It's an intervention," Andy offers, getting up from her bar stool, and I pinch my temples. "Liv is getting over the latest asshole to make her feel like she's not worthy of love."

"Andy," I snap. I don't really need to air all my dirty laundry to two virtual strangers. "It's not that," I correct, following the group to a booth in the back. "I just met someone, and it turns out we weren't on the same page. No big deal."

"That guy, Owen?" Liam asks as we scoot around into the booth. "We met him in the building earlier."

"Yeah," Cal agrees, "Seemed like a decent guy, friends with Eli upstairs, right? But he's an asshole?"

"He's not an asshole," I sigh, unsure how to explain it. "It's just...complicated."

"It usually is," Liam says, lifting his beer bottle in a toast.

"So," Andy starts, folding her hands under her chin and resting her elbows on the table. "They agreed to fake date, because Liv's mom really is an asshole. But then it seemed like maybe the feelings weren't fake after all, so they decided to try a real date, but then maybe the feelings were fake?" Andy ends her summary sounding as confused as I feel. "He also filled her out like an application."

Liam chokes on a sip of beer, and I bury my face in my hands.

"So you're not sure if this was a fake date, a one-night stand—"

"Two!" Andy adds helpfully.

"—a two-night stand or something more?" Cal asks, clearly more used to Andy's antics than poor Liam.

"Basically."

"Did you ask him?"

"Ask him what?" I stare at Cal incredulously.

"If he was just helping you out, having a good time, or likes you for real?"

"Like, 'Hey, were we just hooking up, or do you want something more?'"

"Um," Cal nods, "Yeah, I mean, then you know, right?"

"Straight shooter," Andy nods, "I like your thinking, Cal. Why beat around the bush when you could just jump in it?"

"I don't—" Liam looks at her quizzically, "—get that analogy?"

"Yeah, but what if he thinks I was a mistake?" I ask no one in particular.

"Liv has a bit of past relationship baggage," she stage whispers to the guys.

Liam lifts his beer bottle again. "Don't we all?"

"I just don't want to be some girl he thinks he can fix. I don't want to go down that path again. I'm just not sure it's worth it to try."

Liam leans back, beer bottle resting against his knee. "I don't wanna be that guy who talks in sports metaphors about love," he says with a self-deprecating grin. "But look—I've played baseball my whole life. You know what makes a great hitter? Failing seven out of ten times. And still showing up at the plate like you've got a shot. It's not about getting it right every time. It's about showing up, swinging anyway." He pauses, then adds, a little quieter, "People only remember the home runs, you know? Not all the strikeouts it took to get there."

Cal looks at him with something that looks like a cross between pity and admiration, and I know there is a story there, but I'm too caught up in my misery to ask for details. I stare into the bottom of my empty bourbon glass like it might hold the answers.

"You don't have to figure it all out tonight," Cal says gently.

"Sometimes the best thing you can do is stop, take a breath, and see if the path's still waiting for you in the morning. If it is...then it's real," Liam adds. His voice is quiet, but something in it feels knowing. Like maybe he's learned that the hard way.

Chapter 16

Owen

I stare at the flight board in the American terminal at DFW. My connecting flight home to Santa Barbara, which was already delayed by two hours, was now canceled.

Fuck.

I'm exhausted. My back hurts from five nights in a crappy hotel bed just outside the beltway. Senator Langford was so busy that I hardly had any time to nail down the details of her memoir. It was a wasted trip.

And I hadn't talked to Liv since she left my hotel room Monday morning. I had wanted to text her back or call her a million times, but her last message was pretty clear.

I think it's best if we call this what it was.

If I'm calling it what it was, I thought it was the start of something real, something special. Something unlike anything I'd ever felt before. But it clearly wasn't that for Liv. Maybe my sister was right; maybe I just chase the unavailable damsel in distress, fixing her problems while creating my own. Maybe she just needed a fake date after all.

I dig through my computer bag for my phone, but my fingers catch on a small, lumpy piece of plastic. I pull out the Princess Peach figurine I won for Liv at the arcade, turning it over in my hand. I'd found it on the hotel floor in San Francisco before I checked out and slipped it into my bag, planning to give it back to her that night, back when I thought I'd see her again.

I had only won enough tickets to get her this dumb little toy, but she said it was perfect. Princess Peach stood with her plastic-gloved hands on her pink-gowned hips, and Liv said she was standing in the "power pose," standing tall with feet apart and hands on hips—that signals self-assurance. She said it would be a perfect addition to her desk because it would remind her that when you hold your body like you believe in yourself, your brain often follows.

I've rushed into things before, convinced they were real—until they weren't. But Liv...she felt different. Maybe I'm just telling myself that because I want it to be true. I don't know if this thing between us is everything I think it is—but I know I won't stop wondering if I don't try. Maybe I need to get over my fear and just call her...if I ever get home to Santa Barbara.

"American Airlines Flight 3476 to San Francisco will begin boarding now. Group one, you're welcome to board."

My head snaps up to the gate in front of me, then back down to Princess Peach in my hand.

I've made dumber calls for worse reasons. And if she slams the door in my face, fine. At least I'll know.

I take a deep breath, spread my legs a little wider, and put my hands on my hips, not caring that I'm standing like Superman in the Dallas airport.

Then I go beg the gate agent to rebook my flight.

Chapter 17

Liv

I check my app. My sleep score is perfect.

I mean, my sleep score is shit, I haven't slept in days. But the app tracked it flawlessly—better than any of the prototypes ever did.

"Good morning, Liv. Your sleep score has been consistently low for a few days. Would you like some tips to improve it?"

I bet it was. Launching this app with a broken heart will do that to a girl. I tap *"Sure."*

"Try limiting screen time before bed."

"Reduce alcohol and sugar intake in the evening."

"Maintain a consistent bedtime routine."

"Would you like another suggestion?"

I sigh, "Why not," and tap *"Yes."*

"Reach out to someone you care about. Tell them how you feel. A heart-to-heart can ease emotional stress and improve sleep."

"Stupid bot," I groan and shove the phone into my pocket.

There's a small knock at the door, and I hope it's the food I ordered. I wasn't sleeping, living off DoorDash, and I can't remember the last time I showered. I could pretend it was the launch, but if I'm being honest, I miss Owen.

This week was the most intense of my life, and all I wanted was to share it with him. I wanted to vent when an intern left a fake testimonial on the launch page, and I wanted to celebrate when we doubled our download projections in the first twenty-four hours. When the servers crashed on day three and I ended up crying in the bathroom—something I never let anyone see—I wanted him to be the one to hold me.

I wanted him to see it all. The wins, the mess, the real me.

But I was afraid I'd already ruined it. Whatever this fragile thing was between us, I was scared I'd broken it before it even had a chance. I didn't know if he was back from DC yet, and I hadn't worked up the nerve to call.

Because I'm not sure if he wants the real me, and if he said no...I'm not sure I could handle that either.

I pull open the door, but no one's there. When I glance down, there's no delivery—just a tiny pink figurine. My Princess Peach, striking her power pose. I bend down and pick her up.

"My sleep score has been shit," a warm voice says from across the lobby.

"Owen?" my voice croaks out. He's leaning against the doorframe of the apartment across the hall. Deep purple beneath his eyes, his hair a mess, and his usually crisp button-down is rumpled and slightly untucked. He looks like I feel.

"My bot told me to improve my sleeping conditions," he says, taking one tentative step towards me. "I think it's saying I'd sleep better with you in my bed."

"I'll have to talk to the designer. It sounds like a bug."

"I think it's pretty accurate," he says, and the faint blush I love crawls across his cheek. "Plus, thirty thousand people who've downloaded the app this week agree with me."

"How do you know how well the launch did?"

"I told you," he says, stepping closer but still out of reach. "I like to be prepared...especially when I'm about to sell myself to a prospect."

"Okay," I smile, despite my hammering heart and my clammy palms. "Let's hear it."

"I rush into things. I've tried to fix everything for everyone my whole life. I like to save the day—even when no one asks me to." He looks down for a moment, jaw tight, then lifts his eyes to mine. "But you? You don't need fixing. You're already everything. That's how I know this is different. All I want is to be the one who gets to stand beside you, exactly as you are."

"I accidentally eavesdropped on your call with your sister," I confess.

He nods, but he doesn't look angry, just...relieved. "I wondered."

"You said maybe this was fake." I point my finger back and forth between us.

"We might have started out faking it, but Liv—" he takes another step closer, his voice steady now, eyes fixed on mine, "—every single thing I've said or done while I've been with you has been one hundred percent real.

"At the bar, I didn't step in because I thought you needed saving. I pretended to be your husband because I was already drawn to you and knew you were completely out of my league." His hand lifts, but stops short. "I didn't say yes to the fake engagement because you were desperate. I did it because I would have done anything to spend more time with you.

"And every moment we spent together, it got harder to not want more of that. More of you. That was never fake."

"Owen," my voice shakes a little, and my eyes get glassy with tears. "I've spent so long hiding from anything real—because it always felt so hard. But you...you make it feel easy. Like I don't have to fight so damn hard to be enough. Like you see all of me, and still stay. With you, I feel like I can finally breathe."

He steps closer, but he's still just out of reach.

"I can picture a future with you—not because I want to rush, but because it's so easy it almost hurts. Everything just...makes more sense with you in it."

He lets out a shaky breath, then smiles faintly.

"I want to see you in yellow—hell, I'd paint a whole house yellow for you. I want to eat fried food and let you annihilate me at video games. I want to drive with the top down and curl up to binge shows we only watch together. I want you to teach me about cognitive load reduction, and I want to memorize every little sound you make when I touch you. I'll stand up to your mother, and I'll learn to surf with your brother. I want to know every goddamned thing about you—the messy, the imperfect, the real."

His eyes hold mine, and I can't look away.

"You don't have to fit anyone else's idea of perfect. I'll spend as long as you'll let me proving that to you." His voice catches, raw and unguarded. "Because to me... the real you is perfect."

A strangled sob escapes me at the end of his speech, and I reach out. He takes my hand without hesitation, twines our fingers, and kisses the spot my fake Chinatown ring used to sit.

"I don't want to be your fake husband or your fake fiancé or your fake boyfriend or even a very real hook up," he says. "I want to just be Owen. And I want you just to be Liv, and we'll see where it goes. I want to start over and do it the way I wanted to from the beginning, the real way." He drops my hand and takes a deep breath before looking back up at me. "Hi," he says, his cheeks flushed and his hand outstretched. "I'm Owen. I saw you across the bar, and I was hoping I could buy you a drink."

I laugh and nod my head. "Okay, but I really want to kiss you right now."

"Oh, Button, then let's stop faking it and start something real."

Epilogue

Owen

"Isn't that your neighbor's friend, Liam?" I ask from our booth at Bar None.

"Yeah," she says. "He looks like he could use a friend." We watch as he tips his beer back before gesturing to the bartender to refill his shot glass.

"We are not going to rush in and save everyone who looks a little distressed at a bar," I laugh. "That rarely ends well."

"Sometimes it ends very well," she muses.

We clink our bourbon glasses together and each take a sip. I lean over and give her a quick kiss.

"I like the way you taste," I tell her.

"I like it when you taste me," she says, smirking and taking another sip of her drink.

"Ugh," I groan. "How long is Andy gone tonight? We should go back to your place right now."

"Her parents were in town for the night, so she went to watch their show."

"Their show?" I ask, nipping at the soft skin under her jaw, the way I know she loves.

"She had sort of an unconventional upbringing," she breathes, distracted by my kisses. "But she's probably home by now. Besides, we have barely left that apartment for a week."

I can't believe it's only been a week since I showed up on her doorstep. It feels like a lifetime I've been devoted to this woman. I haven't been back to Santa Barbara now for weeks, and as much as I don't mind living out of a suitcase, I do have to go back tomorrow. Then out to DC again, before coming back here. Back to Liv.

"You know, that apartment across the hall from us is still vacant," she says, cupping my face and kissing me again.

"I thought we weren't going to rush things?" I tease, but my heart is hammering at the prospect of having a more permanent spot here. In San Francisco, near Eli, but most of all, near her. My thoughts swirl with daydreams of early morning oat milk lattes together and trips to the farmer's market in the Ferry Building.

While Liv is right that we have spent most of the past week tangled up in each other, we did finally walk across the Golden Gate Bridge, and I smiled and took pictures like an idiot tourist the whole way. It was great. I want more of it.

"Oh," she reached into her pocket. "I've been meaning to give this back to you." She slides the Chinatown engagement ring from when we were faking it across the table. I looked down at the ring and up to her face. "I just thought..." she stammers, seeing the hurt I was trying to hide. "Now that we're really dating, I should give back the fake engagement ring."

I thought about my sisters telling me not to rush things, to give her a little space. But here she was, the one already hinting at moving in together, while I was trying to take it slow. But I also boarded a plane here with no idea if she'd agree to see me again, and that worked out okay.

"I'll tell you what," I say, picking up the ring and placing it back in her hand. "Why don't you hang on to it, and if at some point you want to, let me know, and we'll trade it for a real one?" I close her fingers around the ring and face forward, taking a sip of bourbon.

Out of the corner of my eye, I see her spinning the ring and biting her lip slightly, the way I've quickly learned is her nervous tell. Maybe I overstepped and pushed too far. But I also know we'll be okay. We can talk about it, share our concerns, and be real with each other. We can share our fears and push back when it's too much for either of us. We won't break.

"I don't know," she says, and my throat tightens a little at the question in her voice. "I kinda like this one." She slips it back on her left hand and holds it out to inspect the glittery bauble. I watch her with the ring—my ring—and I know I can't wait for her to wear one for real. But I meant what I said: whenever she's ready.

"I think this is the real one," she finishes and picks up her drink, leaving the ring in place.

"Like..." I stammer, "Like it's the real one right now?"

"Yeah. You're not the only one who knows what she wants when it's right in front of her."

Thank You!

Thank you so much for reading this novella. If you liked it, please consider leaving a review on Amazon, Goodreads or your own socials. Please tag me @ajclaremontwrites.

And if you want sneak peeks, bonus chapters, and behind-the-scenes on my writing journey, subscribe to my newsletter at www.ajclaremont.com

More in the Across the Hall Series

Crashing Together (Out Now!)
Kiss & Break Up (Spring 2026)
Sleep On It (Summer 2026)
Off the Market (TBD)

Crashing Together

Want more from the residents Across the Hall?

Download Book 2:
Crashing Together

Brother's best friend. Only one bed.
They promised to keep it platonic.
They lied.
Now they're *Crashing Together*.
...Turn the page for a sneak peek!

Chapter 1

Liam

I always thought rock bottom would feel more dramatic. Turns out, it just smells like warm beer and regret.

"You don't have to go home, kid," Frankie says without looking up from where he's wiping down the bar. "But you can't stay here."

I didn't have a home to go home to. That's why I'd been at this dimly lit bar every night since Cal took off for Cambodia a week and a half ago. Or maybe it was Cancun, somewhere with palm trees and no cell service.

Most nights end the same: Frankie kicking me out, me stumbling back to Cal's apartment, collapsing face-first into his bed, and sleeping until either the woman across the hall screams into her phone on her way to work, or I have to piss badly enough to crawl out from under the covers.

Technically, I did have a home. I grew up twenty minutes from here. My mom still lives in the same house, still has my trophies on a shelf. But I hadn't told her I was back in town yet. I hadn't told anyone, aside from Cal, that the Iron Cats let me go and that my big league dreams had quietly died somewhere on a half-lit field in Reno. I sure as hell hadn't told my mom I was crashing at my best friend's apartment and drinking myself numb every night trying not to think about how badly I'd screwed it all up.

I toss two twenties on the bar, but Frankie comes over and slides the bills back toward me.

"I'll put your drinks on Cal's tab," he says, turning to re-shelve bottles before I can object. I put the bills back in my pocket because, let's be honest, I'm in no place to argue.

Minor league baseball players barely make minimum wage, so I'd made ends meet by doing the other players' taxes—I have a weird brain for numbers. I used to tell myself I'd pay off my mom's mortgage once I hit the big leagues, finally repay her for everything she gave up for me. But that dream was as flat as the last sip of beer in this bottle.

I let out a long sigh and figure I should head back to Cal's. I'm not really sure what to do with myself these days. My entire life, since I was fourteen, has revolved around baseball—grueling training, a perfect diet, and studying the game like my life depended on it. Because let's face it, every day you're trying to get called up feels like the most important test you'll ever take. I have zero hobbies, hardly any friends, and I barely even date. Scratch that—I don't date. I don't have time.

I push off the stool and head for the door when a brunette in a strappy tank top and denim skirt gives me that look—the one I know well. The one I've seen in countless bars and hotel lobbies across the US. I've been an athlete my whole life, and I have a face that apparently works in my favor. I might not have time for actual relationships, but I know that without much effort, I could take her home or find a dark corner here. I know my reputation, and honestly, most women seem to want exactly what I have time for—one night, no complications, usually that works for everyone involved.

But even that doesn't sound appealing right now.

Besides, once she finds out I'm just a washed-up ex minor leaguer with a pretty face and not her ticket to the WAG lifestyle, she probably won't want to waste her time anyway. Hell, I'm technically homeless right now. As soon as I was cut, I broke my lease on the apartment I could never really afford anyway. I packed the stuff I cared about into two duffel bags—both of which are still unpacked on Cal's living room floor—and left El Paso to come back to San Francisco.

I give her a tight nod and push through the bar doors to the chilly night. Now, here I was, on the sidewalk in front of Bar None, mooching off my childhood best friend's generosity and wallowing in self-pity. I need to figure out a job, a place to live, and what the fuck I'm doing with my life besides being a has-been ball player with a bruised ego and a mountain of debt.

But that's a problem for tomorrow.

By the time I reach Cal's front door, my vision is so blurry I can barely make out the keypad. But somehow, I manage to stumble into the darkened apartment, strip off my jeans and hoodie, toss them onto the bed, and then collapse face-first into it.

Pretty sure I pass out before my head even hits the pillow.

Chapter 2

Sophie

Cal: *Sophie, if you ever need a place to crash, you can always come to my place.*

I reread the three-month-old text from my brother and hope his offer still stands. Not that I could call to confirm, since he was off somewhere saving the world while my life was falling apart. Typical. I quickly wiped the tears forming in the corners of my eyes.

I shift the duffle bag full of everything I own higher on my shoulder and adjust my grip on the roll of canvases. My grandmother's old art supply box weighs down my other arm—my prized possession, even if it's been gathering dust for months. I start up the stairs, trying to be quiet so as not to disturb Cal's neighbors.

It has to be close to 3 a.m., but I couldn't sleep in my cramped house anymore. Not while my *boyfriend*—or, as he insisted on being called, my *emotional co-creator*—was fucking one of our roommates in the next room, possibly two of them. To be fair, he *had* invited me to join, but I'd told him a thousand times I wasn't into that. But according to him, "monogamy is a tool of capitalism," and my refusal was "a trauma response rooted in ownership culture." Also, I was apparently failing to honor his "universal desire to have his body worshiped by multiple lifeforms." I had my bags packed by the time he reached his "spiritual climax affirmation."

It's called a fucking orgasm, dude—not that he'd ever given me one.

So I drove the ninety minutes from Santa Cruz to San Francisco, circled for twenty minutes to find street parking, and lugged my entire life inside. By the time I hit the landing in front of Cal's apartment, my arms were burning, my heart was broken, and I had exactly zero regrets.

I punched in the door code—our mom's birthdate—and went inside.

It was pitch black, and my heart sank a little as I confirmed I was alone. But what had I expected? Cal was in Cambodia for twelve weeks, and I hadn't seen him in six months. Not since we met for dinner and he tried to talk me out of my current living and romantic situation, saying he was worried about me. What was new? Everyone had been telling me what to do since I was ten years old, and people figured out I could draw a little better than the average fifth grader.

I told Cal that he didn't need to worry, that I could make my own decisions. I was in love with Marshall and enjoyed communal living with a rotating door of roommates in a two-bedroom shithole cabin in the Santa Cruz mountains, and I wasn't attached to material things like he was. He just nodded and told me that if I ever changed my mind, his place was always available.

As I stand in his darkened apartment, I must admit that I *am* looking forward to enjoying some of his material things: consistent hot water, a dishwasher, and most of all, his king-sized bed with its ridiculously high thread count sheets.

I consider taking a shower, but suddenly I'm overwhelmed with fatigue. I think the rush of anger and adrenaline is draining from my body, and everything is catching up with me. I can barely keep my eyes open. I'll crash in Cal's bed tonight and sort everything else out in the morning.

I stumble into Cal's room and don't even have the energy to dig out my pajamas that I'd stuffed into my duffel. I strip down to my underwear and pull on Cal's hoodie, which he'd left at the end of his bed, and climb in.

I'm asleep before my head hits the pillow.

Acknowledgements

To Jen, for reading the very first chapter and giving me your stamp of approval, and more importantly, for the three decades of friendship I'd be lost without.

To Meg, writing can be a weirdly lonely place. I'm so lucky I have you in my back pocket. You are smart, thoughtful and definitely my secret weapon.

To Brooke, Mary and Amy, thank you for the beta reads and the millions of questions I've thrown your way.

To my parents, who always ask me how my books are coming, even though you are not allowed to read this one.

And to Erik for always believing in whatever hairbrained scheme I come up with, like being a romance author.

About the Author

AJ Claremont writes contemporary romance packed with flirty banter, swoony heroes, and enough spice to make you fan yourself while you read.

Her stories are full of women who are both fearless and flawed, and men who are devoted but delightfully complicated — because the best love stories are never simple.

Fueled by coffee, 90s hip hop, and an endless imagination, AJ lives in Northern California with her real-life swoony husband, their two awesome teenagers, and an ever-growing TBR stack.

Keep up with AJ at ajclaremont.com or @ajclaremontwrites on Instagram